OP lst 12⁵ᶜ

Murder Most Irregular

Murder
Most
Irregular

A Novel
by H. Paul Jeffers

St. Martin's Press
New York

Grateful acknowledgment is made to Dame Jean Conan Doyle
for permission to use the characters created by Sir Arthur Conan
Doyle.

Copyedited by Amit Shah

Library of Congress Cataloging in Publication Data

Jeffers, H. Paul (Harry Paul), 1934–
    Murder most irregular.

    "A Joan Kahn book."
    I. Title.
PS3560.E36M8 1983   813'.54   83-9702
ISBN 0-312-55313-7

First Edition
10 9 8 7 6 5 4 3 2 1

To Steve Birnbaum

Contents

"To give your life, or any significant part of it, to the study of Sherlock Holmes is to defy reason."
——Clive James, "The Sherlockologists"
New York Review of Books
February 20, 1975

PROLOGUE
The Game's Afoot

The Sherlock Holmes game has been afoot for more than half a century. It is played primarily by adult males and it rests on the proposition that Sherlock Holmes and Dr. John H. Watson were real men and not simply the literary creatures of Sir Arthur Conan Doyle. If the unwary, the uninitiated, or the unwise suggest that the central figures of the game never existed they will be answered with a cold and steely Holmesian gaze and a flush of anger in Sherlockian cheeks. In extreme cases there might be a challenge to step out-of-doors to settle the matter with fisticuffs. Moderate players of the game are likely to respond with a knowing smile or a clucking of the tongue as an expression of sympathy for the unenlightened doubter. The truly erudite Holmesian might quote Vincent Starrett, one of the earliest players and one of the best writers on the subject: "Shall they not always live in Baker Street? Are they not there this moment as one writes? Outside, the hansoms rattle through the rain, and Moriarty plans his latest devilry. Within, the sea coal flames upon the hearth and Holmes and Watson take their well-won ease. So they will live for all that love them well: in a romantic chamber of the heart, in a nostalgic country of the mind, where it is always 1895."

The four full-length novels and fifty-six short stories
that constitute the life and adventures of Sherlock
Holmes are known as The Canon. These Sacred Writings have appeared in so many editions as to be almost
incalculable, but if Holmes has been a perennial in publishing he has been even more popular as an inspiration
to motion-picture makers. Holmes has been played by
sixty-one actors in one hundred and seventy-five films,
far more than any other character, real or imagined.
"The whole Sherlock Holmes saga," wrote Christopher
Morley in an introductory essay to a compendium of
The Canon, "is a triumphant illustration of art's su-
premacy over life."

In the Sacred Writings, it is through the eyes and the
words of Dr. John H. Watson that readers come to know
Holmes and to peek into his rooms on Baker Street. A
client climbs seventeen steps to 221–B to consult
Holmes but the adventures unfold all over London and
the English countryside with occasional excursions to
the Continent. In all the adventures the reader, like
Watson, is constantly instructed by the sleuth of Baker
Street in the art and science of deduction. Great mys-
teries are unwound through the observance of trifles
while the process is dismissed offhandedly by Holmes
with a word. "Elementary," he cries to Watson in *The
Crooked Man.* "It is one of those instances when the
reasoner can produce an effect which seems remarkable to his neighbour, because the latter has missed the
one little point which is the basis of the deduction."

Watson is a physician because A. Conan Doyle was
one. Eking out meager returns from his practice, he
decided to turn his hand to writing but with little success until he concocted a private consulting detective

who possessed the same remarkable traits of deductive reasoning which Conan Doyle had noticed in a former teacher. Dr. Joseph Bell was a thin, wiry, dark man with a high-nosed acute face, penetrating gray eyes, angular shoulders, and a peculiar walk. "He would sit in his receiving room," wrote Conan Doyle, "with a face like a red Indian, and diagnose the people as they came in, before they even opened their mouths. He would tell them their symptoms, and even give them details of their past life; and hardly ever would he make a mistake."

Later, Conan Doyle's immortal Holmes would instruct Watson, "By a man's finger-nails, by his coat-sleeve, by his boot, by his trouser-knees, by the callosities of his forefinger and thumb, by his expression, by his shirt-cuffs—by each of these things a man's calling is plainly visible." Watson was invariably befuddled and astounded when Holmes demonstrated the effects of pure deductive reasoning. The wonder persisted for years after Watson's first encounter with Holmes in a laboratory of St. Bartholemew's Hospital. A mutual friend had introduced him to Holmes because both men were looking for someone to split the cost of renting rooms. "You have been in Afghanistan, I perceive," said Holmes, quite accurately. That introduction launched one of the great friendships and collaborations in all literature.

Conan Doyle died in 1930. His last Holmes story had been published a few years earlier. Today, for millions of old readers and thousands of new ones all over the world, Holmes remains as vivid and alive as the day Conan Doyle first took up his pen to fill-in lonely hours when patients did not come to his medical consulting rooms. It was ironic that Englishmen who shunned Arthur Conan Doyle as a physician thronged to him through the Sherlock Holmes adventures which they read in *The Strand* magazine. Often, Conan Doyle tried to rid himself of Holmes in favor of other writing, other interests, but Sherlock Holmes's public could not be requited. Always, they wanted to hear the footsteps coming up the stairs to 221–B. The readers of Watson's accounts of Holmes's adventures have remained insatiable.

Starrett described the allure in *The Private Life of Sherlock Holmes:* "Let us speak of the realities that do not change, of that higher realism which is the only true romance. Let us speak, and speak again, of Sherlock Holmes. For the plain fact is, gentlemen, that the imperishable detective—I hope I have said this before— is still a more commanding figure in the world than most of the warriors and statesmen in whose present existence we are invited to believe."

From persuasive clues cited in numerous studies of The Canon it is deduced that Sherlock Holmes was born on Twelfth Night in 1854. Accordingly, every year on the Friday night nearest to January 6 in a hotel on upper Park Avenue in New York City there is a convocation of the most famous and prestigious of the organizations dedicated to the study of the Sacred Writings— the Baker Street Irregulars.

I

The Men of Tor

1
Twelfth Night

"**I** hope you are not going to wear one of those ridiculous caps?"

David Morgan paused in his struggle with his pre-knotted black bow tie to scowl at Nicole Varney in the mirror. "Those ridiculous caps, as you call them, are known as deerstalkers. No, I am not wearing one, although I have one. Nor am I going to put on an Inverness cloak." His tone was as waspish as hers. Their row had been going on for most of the afternoon. "You know I go to the B.S.I. dinner every year." He concentrated on the bow tie again. The suspenders of his tuxedo hung in loops at his hips. As in previous years, he had rented the tuxedo from Mel's Formal Wear on Lexington Avenue. Although tuxedos were not required at the dinner, he had begun wearing one the year following his Investiture under the name Wilson Hargreave, the New York police detective mentioned by Sherlock Holmes in *The Adventure of the Dancing Men*. His certificate of Investiture in the Baker Street Irregulars and the shilling coin which accompanied it were carefully framed and ostentatiously hung in his office next to his license as a private investigator. "I can never get these damned bow ties adjusted to the right length," he growled in exasperation.

3

Nicole studied Morgan from the back. "Be a radical. Take me along to the dinner." Now she was goading. "For crissakes, Nicky, I told you the rule."

"Women not allowed. Outrageous."

Morgan coaxed a peacemaking smile. "It's tradition."

Nicky flounced her long brunette hair. "It's a lousy tradition." She waved a cigarette Bette Davis-fashion and sulked.

"There is one woman who's allowed to come. She represents Irene Adler. In *A Scandal in Bohemia,* Irene Adler got the better of Holmes. After that whenever he referred to Irene Adler it was as *the* woman. Every year a woman is admitted to the cocktail party before the dinner. We drink a toast to her as *the* woman and she is promptly escorted out."

"Positively Neanderthal."

Morgan turned, his tie sagging below his chin. "Darling, you are being downright childish."

"Childish? Look at you. All dressed up for this ridiculous charade. And look at this apartment."

Morgan glanced around. His living room was crowded with book shelves along one wall while the others were festooned with picture frames containing posters, photographs, drawings, paintings, and every other conceivable reminder of the sleuth of Baker Street. "I think my place is quite cozy and inviting."

"A museum to a person who never existed," snapped Nicky.

"You can get an argument about that, Nicky."

"Really, it's preposterous. Grown men playing a laughable charade." She stood and then paced the room, pausing a moment before an oil portrait of Sher-

lock Holmes against the background of a murky fog-
shrouded London street. Atop a table beneath the
painting stood an array of Morgan's pipes in a long
wooden rack. She took one and fingered it.

"Are you going to pick on me for being a smoker as
well as a Sherlockian?"

Nicky replaced the pipe. "It's one of your more in-
gratiating quirks, actually. I like the aroma of pipe tobacco."

Morgan laughed. "Score one point for my side."

She turned. "Pipes are manly. Your hobbies are childish. Sherlock Holmes, toy trains—"

"Model trains, please." He was frowning.

Nicky moved away from Morgan's pipe collection
and strolled past the wall with the book shelves, running a fingertip along the spines of the books. "Who
writes these books?"

"Nicole, some of the greatest men of our time, some
of the best writers in the world, have been Sherlockians. Franklin D. Roosevelt was a Baker Street Irregular!"

"Childish nonsense."

"If you don't understand, I can't explain."

"Of course not. How could a mere woman grasp the
meaning?"

"You're being a bitch, Nicky. When you're being a
bitch you pick on my hobbies. Holmes. The trains. Why
the hell do you bother with me at all?"

"Sometimes I wonder."

"Look. I'll take you out tonight, okay?" He flashed a
smile. "The B.S.I. dinner'll be over by eleven o'clock.
Then you and I can . . ."

"Can what?"

"We can go anywhere you'd like and I'll drink a toast to *the* woman in my life."

"*The* woman is leaving. Don't bother to call me later. I won't be at home." Scooping up the red fox fur jacket he had bought her for Christmas, she strode to the door. The slam of it rattled the things on his walls as she went out.

Morgan stared at the door. "What the hell do women want?"

"The motives of women are so inscrutable. You remember the woman at Margate whom I suspected because she had no powder on her nose? That proved to be the solution. How can you build on such quicksand? Their most trivial action may mean volumes, or their most extraordinary conduct may depend upon a hairpin or a curling-tong."

"Women have changed since your day, if you'll forgive the impertinence."

"Nonsense. It is part of the settled order of Nature that woman's heart and mind are insoluble puzzles to the male. Murder might be condoned or explained, and yet some smaller offence will rankle. A man's hobbies. The way he wears his tie. His social clubs."

Turning to his mirror, Morgan resumed the battle of the bow tie until, miraculously, he found the proper length for the neckband. Slipping into his tuxedo jacket, he admired the deft fit provided by Mel's tailor. A moment later there was a knock on the door. Opening it, he expected to find Nicky but discovered, in-

stead, the enormous hulk known among the Baker
Street Irregulars as B. Alexander Wiggins.

"Wiggy!"

Wiggins pushed into the room and seemed to fill it.
"It's murder, Morgan. Nothing less than murder."

2
Wiggins

"**M**urder?"

"Precisely." Wrapped in layers of coats, sweaters,
and scarves, Wiggins seemed gargantuan—far larger
than Morgan remembered him. Standing in the center
of Morgan's living room while surveying it, studying
the odd assortment of furniture which decorated it,
Wiggins said, "I called at your office. That youngster
. . . your associate . . ."

"Kenny West."

"Yes. He said you had taken the afternoon off. There
was an insinuation that you had slunk away somewhere
with a woman." Wiggins selected a sturdy leather
couch and settled upon it. Through a circular opening
in the swathing of knitted scarves that encased Wiggins's enormous head Morgan found a round face
turned pink by January winds. "I presume, Morgan,
that the beauty who brushed past me as I exited the

elevator was the woman in question. I have no idea what you could have said to send her fleeing in anger. Unless it was to tell her firmly that women are not permitted to attend the annual dinner? There was venom in her eyes, Morgan. I remind you of Holmes's admonition in the Sacred Writings. 'Women are never to be entirely trusted—not the best of them.' "

Morgan found a chair near Wiggins and sat cautiously, mindful of not creasing Mel's tuxedo. "Nicky will calm down. She invariably does."

" 'A man always finds it hard to realize he may have finally lost a woman's love, however badly he may have treated her.' "

Morgan smiled. *The Musgrave Ritual.*

"You needn't prove to me that you know your Canon. After all, it was I who recommended you for B.S.I. membership. How many years ago?"

"Ten."

"You were a tow-headed youth, filled with wonder at being admitted to the inner circle of Sherlockiana." Wiggins smiled benignly, remembering Morgan as a young man seated in intimidated silence at his first Irregulars' dinner. Now, thought Wiggins as he studied his protegé, Morgan was a harder and sharper individual, although he still found traces of the youthful novitiate in Morgan's shock of unruly fair hair, the keen and restless blue-green eyes, the strong jaw, the understated powerful torso. The tuxedo contributed to the aura of lingering youth. Morgan seemed less a shrewd middle-aged detective and more a senior college man heading to a prom. Morgan squirmed self-consciously as Wiggins's eyes loitered upon him and Wiggins was reminded of a puppy which turns its eyes away when stared at. "I'm relieved to have found you at home, Morgan," he said, shifting heavily. "It was vital that I speak to you before you left for the dinner."

"You mentioned the word murder."

The leather couch groaned in protest against its outrageous burden as Wiggins slowly unwrapped his scarves to bare a pumpkin-size head with only tufts of mousey brown hair at ear level. "Only you and I can prevent it." Cobalt eyes barely discernible through slits between meaty cheeks and a ponderous brow fixed on Morgan. "This is not one of the legendary Wiggins pranks, I assure you."

Uncertain, Morgan studied this enormous friend who was as infamous for his rascality as he was celebrated for his Sherlockian expertise. His name—the same as the street urchin who led the band of children in assisting the sleuth of Baker Street, and who were the original Baker Street Irregulars—was suspected by many to be a fraud which Wiggins had succeeded in perpetrating over many years. His reputation as one of the foremost experts on Holmes had provided him with numerous opportunities for pranks as well as for the unmasking of the frauds, phonies, and dilletantes who dared to engage in Sherlockian games. "Who is going to be murdered?" Morgan asked.

"Certain members of the Baker Street Irregulars."

Convinced he was being ribbed, Morgan asked, "How do you know?"

Wiggins moved, dipping a pudgy hand into the folds of his clothing. "Because of this." Producing an envelope, he passed it to Morgan. "The envelope is not in-

structive at all. Cheap five-and-dime stuff. The address
—mine—is typed, probably on a machine in one of
those public typing establishments. Possibly in a library
typing room. It was mailed in New York at the main
post office. The card inside is equally useless in provid-
ing clues. Except for the word scrawled upon it." Morgan withdrew it, a standard-size filing card. The word
was printed in the black ink of a broad felt-tipped pen.
"*Rache,*" said Wiggins. "You will appreciate the signifi-
cance."

"The German word for revenge. It's in *The Sign of
the Four.*"

"Bravo, Morgan."

"It's a joke, Wiggy. A bald joke on the eve of the
annual dinner."

Wiggins slowly shook his head. "Not a joke. You see,
I am not the only Irregular to receive such a threat."
The great head rolled and the deeply-set cobalt eyes
peered intently at Morgan. "All the Irregulars who
hold the Investiture of Man of Tor have received a
card."

"If it's not a joke it's probably just another of the
self-serving little promotionals that we find piled up on
our chairs at every dinner. An Irregular probably has a
new book coming out. This is part of the hype."

"No," sighed Wiggins as he eased forward on the
couch with an air of dejection. "I have proof that it is
not a joke. I happen to know that the first attempt at
murder has already occurred."

"When?"

"Tonight."

"Against whom?"

"Me."

3
The Illustrious Client

Wiggins rolled up the right sleeve of his overcoat and bared his wrist. "The only souvenir I have to show for the inconvenience of being murderously attacked is this scraped arm, I'm afraid. The fellow who wrenched my wrist had on a ring that scratched rather painfully. Otherwise, I am unscathed. Fortunately, the scarves around my head prevented the blows from their sticks from doing any real damage." He smiled. "My head has always been my least vulnerable spot. The two men dashed away without doing any serious harm, although I'm convinced they intended it. They were hired for the job, of course."

"Christ, Wiggy, two men attacked you?"

"With sticks." He chuckled and rubbed his hands together. "Surely that has a familiar sound to it? Attacked on a street with sticks? In *The Adventure of the Illustrious Client* Holmes was set upon in broad daylight in front of Cafe Royal near Piccadilly Circus. That is the instructive part, Morgan." Wiggins drew back and the couch creaked under his weight. He touched steepled fingers to his Cupid's bow lips. "Of course, you are the detective, but this attack seems to prove one thing to me. The Men of Tor are marked for murder and the methods of murder are to be found in the writings of Dr. John H. Watson. The assault on me was drawn from *The Adventure of the Illustrious Client.*

Who knows what adventure has been chosen as the blueprint for the next murder?"

"The attack on you, have you reported it to the police?"

Wiggins groaned. "Morgan, we are living in New York City in the waning decades of the twentieth century. This is not Victorian London. There were no Scotland Yard bobbies strolling your neighborhood ready to race to the rescue of a citizen assaulted on the street. The harried professionals of the New York Police Department would dismiss me as another mugging victim."

"This is a rough neighborhood. Plenty of muggings."

"It would be a very brave man who would choose someone of my dimensions as a mugging victim. I was set upon by two men and I am convinced they were hired by whoever sent that card. This person has a list of Irregulars marked for murder. Those men are known by you."

"The Men of Tor? Yourself, Ben Artnikoff, James Donald Cape, Bill Miner, Ethan Cage Remarque, Cliff Brownglass, and Herman Sloan."

"They will all be at the dinner this evening. You will have a chance to question each of them, of course. I have asked them to bring their own versions of that devilish little card."

"You've told them your theory?"

"They are skeptical but open-minded. They are not unaware of the curious timing of the arrival of these threats. I do not refer only to their coincidence with our annual dinner but with an event which follows it this year."

"What event?"

"On this very weekend, the Men of Tor who have received the cards are scheduled to go to London, a junket into the heart of Sherlock Holmes country."

"Why?"

"Oh, for the commonest of reasons. The making of money. About three months ago we were contacted by a young woman who runs a travel service here in New York. The Lonsback Agency on Madison Avenue. Miss Lonsback acted on instructions from one of the most distinguished Sherlockians in England, Sir Malcolm Bannister. You have some of his books on your Holmes shelf, I'm sure. A very interesting chap. He was born a millionaire and to a title, yet he worked most of his life in the same profession as John H. Watson—a physician. He's retired now and has spent his retirement restoring an old house in Devonshire. He's named it Baskerville Hall. A replica of the house on Dartmoor. Sir Malcolm envisions establishing Sherlock Holmes educational tours. The Lonsback Agency will handle the travel end. Sir Malcolm will be the London host. The Men of Tor will alternate as escorts. We leave for London tomorrow evening to finalize the enterprise. I believe that the person who sent the cards and who orchestrated the assault on me knows our plans and intends to murder the Men of Tor in England."

"You were attacked here."

"It wasn't until yesterday that I agreed to take part in the project. It seemed crass in the extreme at first. Only the continued urgings of the others persuaded me at the last minute to go. And then only with the proviso that if the scheme smacks in the slightest of cheap commercialism with no serious scholarly purpose we will withdraw our support from the enterprise. I have no objection to the Men of Tor profiting, of course, but I will not allow the pilgrimages to become nothing but sightseeing. Serious Sherlockians only need apply. Because it appeared that I would not be going to London, I had to be attacked here. Had I always been on the list of travelers I would not have been assaulted tonight. I would have been targeted to satisfy someone's lust for revenge in London, as the other Men of Tor have been. They are in serious peril, I assure you. That's why you must come to London with us. You must put aside all your cases, all your personal business, and come to Baker Street."

"You need the police, Wiggy. Either the cops here in New York or Scotland Yard in London. I can give you the number of Chief Superintendent Ivor Griffith."

"Scotland Yard would dismiss me as abruptly as the New York police. No, you must investigate this, Morgan."

"My advice is, don't go to London."

"Out of the question. It's too late to cancel. You will not find a Man of Tor who would take that advice. We will not live our lives in fear because of anonymous threats."

"Someone tried to kill you tonight, Wiggy."

"And if we called off the trip to London? How long would it be until we were all murdered in our homes? No. The only way to apprehend the man behind this outrageous plot is to go forward with our plans. Beard him in London. I am positive he is waiting for us. That's why you must come. With one exception, you are the finest private investigator in my experience. I'll arrange everything. You do have a valid passport?"

"I do."

"It's settled then." Wiggins smiled and wrapped his scarf around his thick neck. "Now, off to the Queen Victoria Hotel where we and all the Irregulars will hoist the usual canonical toasts. If we don't rush we'll miss the one to *the* woman."

"There's time for you to tell me the name of the person you suspect is behind this crazy business."

Wiggins could not contain his amusement. "There! You see that I am right in ranking you second only to Holmes in my esteem. Of course I have a suspect! How shrewd of you to deduce it." The pleased smile vanished. "The story goes back to a date long before I had the honor of bringing you into the Irregulars. I and the others—the Men of Tor—were approached to admit a man who turned out to be nothing but a fraud and a charlatan. He went under the name Joseph Bell. Yes, the same name as the Dr. Bell who was the model used by Conan Doyle in his characterization of Holmes. This person calling himself Bell presented us with a considerable pile of scholarship. It consisted of articles from popular magazines, privately printed monographs and the like. Nothing from any of the established Sherlockian journals. It was this which made me suspicious. I unmasked Joseph Bell and refuted his claim to be a descendant of the real Dr. Bell. In a line by line analysis of his so-called writings I proved that he was a consummate copier of other people's works. It was skillfully-done plagiarism of the most audacious kind. We saw to it that Bell was banned from membership in any Sherlockian society. He disappeared after I unmasked him. Now I am convinced that he has surfaced after all these years to seek revenge on those of us who humiliated him. *Rache!*" Wiggins clapped huge hands on bulky knees, then rose. "Now, my friend, we must be off to the Queen Victoria Hotel."

Morgan clutched the collar of his overcoat around his neck as he waited patiently for Wiggins to hail a taxi. The first two vacant cabs passed unhailed. Wiggins frantically waved down the next. Never take the first cab, nor the second; the third will probably be safe: the commandment regarding cabs according to the Sacred Writings. That someone—even Wiggins—would actually obey Holmes's rule amazed Morgan as he squeezed into the narrow space left for him in the back of the taxi. "Queen Victoria Hotel," said Wiggins to the driver.

4

The Third Cab

The appearance of Sherlock Holmes into the life of David Morgan was one of those moments which impress themselves upon the mind and years later replay as if on tape with all the clarity of the day on which they happened. Plunging naked into a slow, deep, cold, brown stream which cut through stands of sweet-smelling corn on either bank, on a day so far in the clouded past no one could remember that other boys had struggled to heave boulders and rocks into place to fashion a dam stemming the flow and widening and deepening the creek, making it suitable for swimming. Coming out of the frigid dark of a double-feature Saturday matinee at the Rialto theater and into the breath-stealing, blinding scorch of August when it seemed that summer would go on forever and the happiness of western shoot-'em-ups and edge-of-the-seat detective thrillers could never end. The dim, damp, chalk-dust-smelling new classroom where, quite abruptly, summer ended and reality returned.

In the cab beside Wiggins, Morgan remembered his first encounter with Sherlock Holmes in such a way. He was ten years old and scouring shelves of musty books in the narrow stacks of the Robinsville branch of the Pennsylvania Public Library in search of the slimmest volume he could find for the purpose of writing a book report for Miss McKeon's reading class. From the line of books whose authors' names began with the letter *D* he drew a slender volume titled *The Hound of the Baskervilles.* The book was encouragingly thin. When he opened it somewhere near the front his eye fell on the captivating last sentence of a chapter. "Mr. Holmes, they were the footprints of a gigantic hound!"

That he became a policeman and subsequently a private investigator was, Morgan believed, the inevitable result of that lazy-spirited selection of a book. Often he wondered what course his life might have taken had he wandered into a row of books whose authors' names began with *F* or *R* or *T*.

"What are you mulling over in that mind of yours?" asked Wiggins. "I hope it's the mystery I've brought to you so unexpectedly."

Morgan glanced at Wiggins in profile. "Farthest thing from my mind."

"Worried about *the* woman in your life?"

Morgan grunted a laugh. "I'd forgotten about her. Funny."

"She is well-forgotten," said Wiggins.

Like his encounter with Holmes in the Robinsville Public Library, Morgan's first meeting with B. Alexander Wiggins was an indelible memory. A Greenwich Village film society had announced a Sherlock Holmes festival which promised to run all of the films made with Basil Rathbone as Holmes and Nigel Bruce as Watson. The highlight of the screenings was to be a showing of the uncensored version of the first of the Rathbone pictures, *The Hound of the Baskervilles,* the final scene of which had been edited by the Hays Office because it showed Holmes turning to Watson with the words, "Oh Watson, the needle." But the film which Morgan yearned to see again was *Pursuit to Algiers* in which Nigel Bruce's winning Scottish accents are heard in a hauntingly sweet rendition of "Loch Lomond." To his delight and amazement, the lecturer who introduced the films, one B. Alexander Wiggins, by far the largest human being Morgan had ever seen, stated, "In this film there is one of my favorite scenes in all the Rathbone-Bruce portrayals of Holmes and Watson. In it, Watson *sings.*"

In such moments, friendships and Holmesian camaraderie are welded.

Morgan again studied Wiggins sidewise as the taxi picked its way through a clog of traffic where the Fifty-ninth Street Bridge disgorged itself upon First Avenue. Anyone would have to be mad to attack such a creature, he thought as the cab idled and Wiggins stared through the window from inside the cocoon of his wintry wrappings. Yet someone had attacked him. Two men—nameless, faceless—had assaulted him, wounded him, meant him serious harm. Had, perhaps, intended to kill him.

The taxi broke through the clog and Wiggins spoke. "The reason they did not succeed when they assaulted me, Morgan, is that I screamed my bloody head off and ran like the dickens. Yes. Amusing as the mental picture may seem to you, I ran. And don't look so amazed that I knew what was in your thoughts. It was elementary deduction. As much as I admire you as a person and a detective, Morgan, there are moments when I wonder how you manage to make a living when the simplest things seem to go by you."

Morgan chuckled. "I don't have much call to use the science of deduction handling divorce cases, Wiggy."

"For the next few days in London you will be relieved of that tedium."

"I haven't agreed to go to London."

"You haven't said you're going, but you'll go."

"I'll talk to the Men of Tor first."

"They will confirm what I've told you. Each is bringing his little greeting card."

Morgan studied the traffic on First Avenue as the taxi made slow progress uptown toward the Queen Victoria Hotel. "The bogus Joseph Bell. Did you ever learn his real name?"

"Oh, his name was Joseph Bell. It was his genealogy that was phony. His branch of the Bell family was the Boston—not the London—variety."

"Tomorrow I'll have Kenny West make a quick check of the Boston Bells."

"It was years ago, Morgan."

"That is exactly why I want to check on Mr. Bell. All

those years, anything could have happened. Bell may
be dead."

"Or alive. And in London."

"Or alive. And in Boston."

"And if he is, it will not erase the fact that the Men
of Tor have received threats in the mail and that I was
murderously attacked tonight in your very neighborhood. It is possible that my suspect—the scurrilous Joseph Bell—is not our culprit. That there is a culprit
. . . waiting for us in London . . . I'm convinced."

The taxi had broken free of traffic, turned from First
Avenue, and was nosing into a driveway that led to the
portico of the Queen Victoria Hotel. In the yellow
lights of the entrance loitered men of all shapes and
sizes and of every age. More than a few of them were
capped with deerstalkers and cloaked in tweed Inver-
nesses. The air was pungent with the aroma of strong
tobacco smouldering in the enormous yellow bowls of
a dozen Calabashes and as many bent black briars.
"There's a strange bunch of characters," growled the
driver. "Looks like a bunch of limeys."

"Quite," grunted Wiggins as he handed the driver
the fare.

Morgan stepped from the cab and joined the
fold. Among the mingling, meandering, chattering,
chuckling, pipe-puffing, deerstalkered, and Inverness-
cloaked Baker Street Irregulars, he felt a rush of excitement and comradeship and understood that any
threat to any of them, or to any group of them, or to
all of them was a threat to him and a desecration of
that inexplicable magic which had graced his boyhood
in the dusty stacks of a library and had remained a
part of him since.

5

The Baker Street Irregulars

Morgan followed the crowd into a long, narrow, and gilded room where the Baker Street Irregulars happily imbibed drinks, renewed friendships, exchanged gossip, and waited for the call from their Commissionaire to hoist their glasses for the first of the evening's toasts. Irene Adler, on this blustering Twelfth Night, was a matronly, giggling, and slightly embarrassed author who had joined the annual ritual despite the certainty that she would be promptly ushered out after the toast while the Irregulars filed into an ornately Victorian dining room for dinner, speeches, revelry, learned papers, reports of the scion societies, presentation of new members, Investitures, mandated rituals, and recitations and toasts to Holmes, Watson, and their patient landlady, Mrs. Hudson. Twelve tables with twelve places awaited the presence of men whom the first editor of the *Baker Street Journal*, Edgar W. Smith, had described as well-rounded, earthly, and generously-sophisticated men for whom it was characteristic to be interested in Sherlock Holmes; to see eye-to-eye with the Baker Street Irregulars in their strength-giving foibles. Among these singular men Morgan was seeking John Edgar Foxx.

Of the one hundred and forty-four roiling and babbling Baker Street Irregulars in the smoke-filled room, many had been attending the conclaves for most of the

five decades of the existence of the premier Sherlockian group but only John Edgar Foxx had been there at
the beginning at Cella's restaurant on the evening of
June 5, 1934, for the first formal meeting of the Irregulars. For present-day Irregulars, Foxx was the spirit, the
living connection to their beginnings, and a walking
history book of the B.S.I.

Searching for him, Morgan felt a pang of pity for
Nicole Varney who would not—or could not—understand what bonded him to the men who jostled him,
blocked him, and waylaid him with greetings and small
talk. A modern liberated woman, Nicole Varney would
never be able to accept his membership in an organiza-
tion which barred women. She would not concede that
it would be out of character for those who held Sherlock
Holmes infallible in all things to admit women to their
yearly obeisance to a man who mistrusted women and
avoided them because, as he told Watson in *The Sign
of the Four*, "Love is an emotional thing, and whatever
is emotional is opposed to that true, cold reason which
I place above all things." Thoughts of, and sympathy
for, Nicole evaporated when Morgan discovered John
Edgar Foxx in a corner of the room, a waiflike figure
shamefully aloof from the swirl of the Sherlockians.
"John Edgar! Good to see you again."

The old man smiled and lifted a glass of sherry in
salute. "Hello, Morgan. You have no drink! You must
put a glass in your hand. We'll be toasting Irene Adler
in a moment. Are you on the program this evening? I
was very much impressed with your reading of *The
Musgrave Ritual* at last year's dinner. I've heard it
every year and not many did it as well as you. Your
rendition ranked with the finest."

"That's quite a tribute, John Edgar."

"I've a mind to speak to our Commissionaire and have him put you on the program next year for the reading of the Constitution and By-laws."

"You had a hand in drawing them up."

"Oh, no. It was Elmer Davis who did that. I was never as clever with words as Christopher Morley or Davis. They wrote the wit into our founding documents."

"They may have provided the wit but you've been the soul of B.S.I., John Edgar."

Flattered, the old man sipped his sherry. Lowering the glass he studied Morgan's face. "There's a glint in your eye. It's a sparkle that comes into a policeman's gaze when he's on the trail of something."

"I am interested in a piece of Irregular history, John Edgar. It was a few years ago and involved a man named Joseph Bell."

The old man frowned. "It was a nasty affair. I remember it very well. The chap was a bit of a deceiver. What brings up that unpleasant episode?"

Morgan shrugged. "Oh, nothing important."

"Ah, I suspect it's very important, but obviously it concerns me only to the extent of confirming that the incident took place. Am I correct?"

"That's it exactly," Morgan said with a grin.

"Then I won't pursue it. Now, young man, fetch yourself a drink."

A moment later, equipped for the occasion with a Scotch and soda, Morgan joined in the toast to *the* woman. "Gentlemen," boomed the voice of the Commissionaire. Silence fell. "Miss Irene Adler," intoned the Commissionaire. Twelve dozen glasses poked toward the ceiling. "Here, here," someone muttered. In the midst of the Irregulars the smiling, blushing, matronly representation of the woman who had bettered Sherlock Holmes basked in the glory. Morgan felt a tug at his sleeve.

"I must speak with you."

Turning, Morgan was face to face with the mutton-chop whiskers of Benjamin Artnikoff.

"Meet me in the gents' room."

6

The Lion's Mane

There were two conceivable rationalizations for Benjamin Artnikoff's Investiture as Fitzroy Macpherson. The obvious one lay in the intellectual similarity between Artnikoff and Macpherson, a science master of a local school in a remote part of Sussex where the older Sherlock Holmes enjoyed his retirement by taking the air along the Channel cliffs. On one of these perambulations, Holmes encountered a dying Macpherson and witnessed the failing man's last words: "The lion's mane." The second explanation for Artnikoff's Investiture lay in the lush growth of gray hair upon Artnikoff's head. If ever a head of human hair could be compared to a lion's mane, it was Artnikoff's. Completing his hirsute appearance was a pair of mutton-chops that, in photographs of the Irregulars which were taken each year as part of the ritual conclave, made Artnikoff look exactly like a whiskered Toby mug. While no official explanations are given for the selection of Investitures, Artnikoff's reputation as a prolific writer in the field of science and science fiction seemed justification enough for giving him his shilling in the name of the hapless intellectual Macpherson. Author of scores of books in addition to his scientific volumes, Artnikoff had become the poet laureate of the B.S.I. No Irregular dinner could be considered complete without Artnikoff swaggering to the rostrum to deliver an ode, a limerick, or a sonnet in boisterous praise or loving mockery of Holmes or the Irregulars or both. Asked on one occasion by a reporter covering the dinner why he was so prolific an author, Artnikoff retorted, "I type fast." Asked what he would do if he were told he had less than a year to live, Artnikoff replied, "Type faster."

Artnikoff was leaning against the wall at the end of a line of urinals when Morgan came into the men's room. "You've spoken with Wiggins?" Artnikoff asked.

Morgan nodded. "You received one of the cards?"

Artnikoff produced it with a flourish from his inside jacket pocket. Handing it to Morgan, he asked, "Are you coming to London with us?"

Morgan fingered the card. The word on it was the same, printed in the same manner with a felt-tipped pen. Idly, Morgan turned over the card, then flipped it over again and stared at it. "What do you make of these curious greeting cards, Ben?"

"At first I thought I was being led on to what I assumed would be a pitch of some kind. A clever bit of advertising in the opening of a campaign to sell me something."

"And now?"

"Now I think someone with a sick mind is up to mischief that won't do anyone any good."

"Wiggy says it's murder."

"Could be."

"You don't seem very upset about being on someone's assassination list." He passed the card back to Artnikoff.

"I'm not the sort to quiver in my boots just because I've gotten an anonymous threat in the morning post." He slipped the card back into his pocket. "I can take care of myself if it comes to that."

"Wiggins has a suspect in mind."

"Joseph Bell?"

"Yes."

Artnikoff made a face. "That is very ancient history. A dozen years is a long time to carry a grudge."

"It's been done before."

"Getting the boot from the Baker Street Irregulars strikes me as a fairly lame motive for plotting the wholesale extermination of the Men of Tor."

"You discount Joseph Bell as a suspect?"

"I don't discount anyone but if I were in the discounting trade I would mark him down quite a bit. Look, the fellows who got these cards have been big boys for a long time. There isn't a name on the mailing list that doesn't have a long row of black marks behind it in the Great Register of Sins. Hell, I could give you my bedside book of frequently-called telephone numbers and at least half of the names in that little black book would have a reason to wish me ill. That is, if they are the kind to carry grudges. I daresay I've bruised or battered all of my best friends through the years. What the hell are

friends for if not to abuse from time to time? Maybe one
of them did take silent extreme umbrage and is now
determined to eradicate me. Who can know?"

"Why would one of your friends go after the others?"

"Well, as I've always said, if you want to kill someone,
kill several people so that your foul deed doesn't attract
undue attention by virtue of there being only one
corpse. Were I to plan a murder I would concoct a
scheme for wholesale killing in the hope that my intended victim would get lost in the crowd. That's probably what's going on in this mysterious *Adventure of
the Cheap File Cards.*"

"Do you know who sent the cards?"

Artnikoff laughed. "There's nothing oblique about
you, Morgan."

"Would you have a suspect in mind?"

"As a matter of fact, I would."

Morgan waited. "Well? Who?"

"Wiggins."

Morgan laughed. "On what evidence?"

"Well, the fellow has always been a bit of a fruitcake.
If all of us have gone off the deep end in this Sherlockian cult of ours, Wiggins is the only one of us who went
off the deep end wearing scuba gear. If we didn't have
this happy little group as a justification for our mild
mental malady we might all be certified loony. Wiggins
would qualify for a rubber room."

"Wiggy's eccentric, not nuts."

"If you say so."

"Why would Wiggy want to kill the Men of Tor?"

"To conceal the fact that he would like to kill *one* of
the Men of Tor. I refer to yours truly."

"I don't believe what I'm hearing."

"It's quite simple. Several years ago we undertook a joint literary venture. It had a Sherlockian connection, of course, but as our discussions with a publisher progressed it became clear to the publisher and to me that Wiggins was drifting away from the original idea. We tried to steer him back on track. It was impossible. Finally, the publisher and I went ahead with the project as we envisioned it. Wiggins was left out in the cold."

"That's hardly grounds for murder."

"In a balanced mind."

"Why would he wait so long?"

Artnikoff shrugged. "I'm a writer not a head shrinker."

"Yet you're going ahead with this Sherlock Holmes-Baker Street tour with Wiggins."

"Oh, yes. The project would collapse without his participation. Nobody argued more strenuously than I to persuade Wiggy to give in and come with us to London to explore Sir Malcolm's project. Wiggy may or may not be nursing a vendetta against me because of one sour incident in our association but that's no reason to jettison a good Sherlockian project." Artnikoff smiled and clapped Morgan on the shoulder. "Anyway, you asked if I had a suspect. I gave you one. My suspicion hardly amounts to an indictment and certainly falls short of a verdict of guilty. I don't envy you in this little *affaire du crime.* There are seven Men of Tor who've gotten cards in the mail. After you've interviewed all of them, I'll wager, you'll have more suspects than you can shake a stick at. No pun intended in connection with the attack on Wiggins tonight." Artnikoff paused before leaving the men's room. "You know, that attack on Wiggins seems quite significant to me."

"It could have been an ordinary mugging."

"That is possible, but it's been my observation that muggers use knives or guns. Not sticks. Curious, isn't it?" He pulled open the door.

"Ben. Is there any reason why I shouldn't consider *you* a suspect?" Morgan was smiling.

Artnikoff shrugged. "No."

7

The Men of Tor

"**T**here you are, Morgan." Wiggins was alone in the long gilded room where the Irregulars had toasted *the* woman. "Where've you been? I was afraid you'd gone home."

"Men's room," Morgan muttered.

"I've done some shuffling of the seating arrangements so that you may join us at table Number One. Come, or they'll snatch away your appetizer before you've had a chance to taste it. You know how irresponsible these waiters are."

The Men of Tor flanked Morgan's chair at the large round table reserved for the ranking members of the Baker Street Irregulars. "We've put you with three Men of Tor on one side and the rest on the other," said Ben Artnikoff, who was already occupied with his shrimp cocktail. "The better to interrogate us." He smiled.

Wiggins found his place while Morgan sat in the spot selected for him. On the other curve of the table, looking amused but vaguely confused, sat five other Irregulars, including the tall, austere, and slightly nervous Commissionaire who would be the evening's master of ceremonies, as always. "What's this little group up to?" he asked.

"Up to no good, I'm sure," said the venerable John Edgar Foxx with a chuckle as he nibbled a shrimp dripping red sauce.

"Maybe we should change their collective name from Men of Tor to the Reigate Squires," said the Commissionaire.

"What about the Six Napoleons?" Ben Artnikoff was smiling.

"There ought to be seven Men of Tor," said Morgan. Surveying the assemblage, he asked, "Where's Herman Sloan?"

The Commissionaire looked up. "Herman's not here?" Perplexed, he glanced around table Number One then craned his long neck to scrutinize the other tables. "Odd. He was among the first to respond to the invitation. He's always prompt with his check. Perhaps his train's late getting into Penn Station."

Wiggins cast a troubled glance at Morgan. "I believe one of us ought to phone Herman's home."

"Nonsense," said the Commissionaire. "Herman will be here. He never misses a dinner."

Wiggins struggled up. "I'm going to call."

As Wiggins barreled between tables on his way to the lobby telephones, James Donald Cape cracked, "First

time Wiggy's ever voluntarily left a dinner table." The
jab provoked laughter around the circle.

Seated to Morgan's left, James Donald Cape toyed
with a soup spoon and basked in the appreciation of his
little joke but when the chuckling faded he leaned toward Morgan and whispered, "That was in bad taste, I
know. But I don't think that we ought to sit here with
sour pusses just because we've all received those cursed
letters. I know Wiggins is worried, and with good reason, in view of the strange absence of one who got a
card. It was good of him to make the call." He patted
Morgan's hand. "When are you coming to my ranch for
some serious horse riding, Morgan? You're overdue."

Cape spoke with a soft Texas drawl that completely
suited his appearance. A large outdoorsy man with
broad square shoulders and an impressively youthful
torso for one over sixty years of age, Cape was a rancher
who had been a genuine cowboy in his youth before
buying his first small cattle ranch in the Texas panhan-
dle. That ranch had grown into one of the largest and
richest landholdings in the Lone Star state. Had his
cattle holdings not made him a millionaire, the petro-
leum reserves lying beneath his ranch would have. The
Cape millions had afforded the devout Sherlockian
more than enough money to assemble the largest collection of Holmesian artifacts, books, and ephemera in
the United States. Affable, generous, and witty, James
Donald Cape attended the Baker Street Irregulars as-
siduously, flying to New York in his private Lear jet and
striding into the Queen Victoria Hotel in western gear
and a deerstalker cap. Morgan liked Cape. "What credence do you put in Wiggy's theory regarding the likely
suspect, Jim?"

"None whatsoever. Arthur Hess-Feldstein is my nominee."

This assertion was overhead by Bill Miner. "Ah, that's ridiculous."

"Makes perfectly good sense," retorted Cape. "The man abominates us."

"Arthur Hess-Feldstein the book critic?" asked Morgan.

"There could be only one Arthur Hess-Feldstein." Ben Artnikoff chuckled. "I hadn't even thought of him. Yes, I'd put him on anybody's list of suspects."

"Fill me in," said Morgan.

Bill Miner seized the floor. "The little Prussian weasel did a hatchet job on those of us who labor in the literary vineyards at the task of keeping the Holmes candle burning. Two years ago in the *National Review of Books* Hess-Feldstein wrote a venomous essay which he cutely titled 'The Adventure of the Conan Doyle Ghouls.' That's us. That's anyone who has ever thought about Holmes and put a sheet of paper in a typewriter to turn out a clever and amusing pastiche."

" 'Literary rip-off,' was Hess-Feldstein's phrase," chimed in Ben Artnikoff across his soup spoon.

"The *raison d'être* for the essay in the *Review* was the publication of Bill's last book," added Cliff Brownglass, a portly Man of Tor whose field of expertise was the films of Sherlock Holmes. "Took the hide off you, Bill."

Miner shrugged slender shoulders.

James Donald Cape leaned toward Morgan. "Bill sued, if you recall. Won in the lower court but was reversed on appeal."

"That's motive for Bill to murder Hess-Feldstein, not vice versa," said Morgan.

"The bastard hates us," announced Cliff Brownglass. "He has never given a favorable review to any of the writers at this table."

The Commissionaire could contain himself no longer. "Murder?"

Morgan smiled at the Commissionaire. "Don't be misled. We're playing a little game here."

"Ah." The Commissionaire nodded. Relieved, he bent over his mushroom soup à la Mrs. Hudson.

"Let us know who wins," said John Edgar Foxx, a bit irritably.

Cliff Brownglass resumed. "In his essay, Hess-Feldstein tore into anyone who ever dabbled in writing about Holmes. I believe he referred to our work as the witless cairn of Sherlockiana. Well, the upshot came when Hess-Feldstein delivered his next manuscript to a publisher. The publisher delivered a scathing lecture in defense of Sherlockianism and rejected Hess-Feldstein's book out of hand. Never cracked the pages. You see, the publisher is a lifelong student of The Canon. Granted, his decision to turn down Hess-Feldstein's manuscript was shockingly unprofessional and very bad business management. But the publisher was livid over what Hess-Feldstein wrote in the essay. Shortly after the critic got short shrift on his manuscript, the *Review* granted equal space to those whom Hess-Feldstein had attacked in its pages. The reply was a cleverly devastating parody of Hess-Feldstein's own columns. The reply was a joint literary effort of—"

"The Men of Tor," said Morgan.

"Hardly a reason to accuse Hess-Feldstein of plotting mass murder," said Bill Miner.

"Yes, I'd be more inclined to suspect you of wanting

to kill Hess-Feldstein." Ethan Cage Remarque spoke up for the first time. Always a quiet and diffident man, the scholarly Remarque had produced an annotated edition of all the Holmes novels and stories and was regarded as one of the most serious and accomplished literary analysts of the work of Sir Arthur Conan Doyle. Slight, balding, bespectacled, and soft-spoken, Remarque was the second-longest member of the Irregulars, having joined two years after John Edgar Foxx.

"What do you make of the cards, Ethan?"

"A prank."

"There's no one in your past who might want to bump you off?"

Remarque dismissed the question with a wave of a long thin hand.

"Not so," Cliff Brownglass said. He took his time sipping dietetic ginger ale. "I detest this swill," he grimaced, setting down the soft drink. "But what is a diabetic to do?"

"Be thankful you're still alive," grunted Ethan Remarque.

"You don't have to stick needles into yourself," snapped Cliff Brownglass. "And as for your enemies . . ."

Remarque muttered, "Stuff and nonsense."

Cliff Brownglass turned to Morgan. "A year ago I was approached by Leslie Westin, a producer for one of the television networks. He had an idea for a TV series based on Holmes. Certain liberties were to be taken."

"Liberties!" Ethan Remarque coughed a laugh.

"Ethan scotched the deal. Probably cost Westin a million or more."

"You might have profited, too," said Remarque, "but

I doubt very much if you would consider murdering me in spite."

"I might." Brownglass chuckled.

Morgan leaned back as a waiter bent over him to take away his unfinished but cold bowl of Mrs. Hudson's mushroom soup. "You fellows have certainly compiled an impressive list of enemies."

"We do our duty," Ethan Cage Remarque said.

The waiter set the main course—listed in the menu as Sherlock Holmes Roast of Beef—before Morgan. A traditional English roast, it was served with horseradish sauce which was ominously listed as Sauce Moriarty, and a Yorkshire pudding appropriately called Baskerville Pudding. Before he could taste the meal, he was summoned from the table by Wiggins looming large in the doorway and frantically waving a thick arm.

"What is it, Wiggy?"

The pumpkin face was ashen. "Herman Sloan is dead."

"Christ. When? How?"

"Late this afternoon. He was on his way to the railroad station on his bicycle." Wiggins paused. "Herman was a convert to physical exercise. Lately, he'd taken to cycling and given up taking his car to the station for his trips into the city in favor of his bike. His body was found about half a mile from his house in Merrick. Shot through the back with a .22 caliber rifle bullet. The police believe it was an accident, an errant shot by someone target shooting in the woods. There'd been the sound of shots off and on during the afternoon. The police are listing it as an accident. Accident! Not a chance. Need I remind you of the means of death in *The Adventure of the Solitary Cyclist?*"

Morgan chewed his lip. "Keep this to yourself for now. No point in ruining everyone's evening."

"This certainly proves that I'm right about the threats, Morgan."

"It proves that I'm right and that you must go to the police."

"There is no time. The drama is going to unfold in London. Everything points to it."

"You were attacked here. Sloan was killed here."

"And tomorrow the rest of us go to London. Unless I am a complete fool, I can assure you that the mastermind of this plot, our own devilish Moriarty, is already on his way to London." Wiggins placed an insistent hand on Morgan's shoulder. "David, you are our only hope. You can't fail us."

Morgan wavered. "When is your flight?"

"Seven o'clock tomorrow evening. One call by me to Miss Lonsback will arrange everything."

Morgan's eyes drifted across the glittering room of the Queen Victoria Hotel. The elegant gold-and-white walls reflected the shimmering light of crystal chandeliers. Tall slim candles flickered at the centers of twelve tables. The boisterous babble of the cocktail hour was now a baritone hum as the Baker Street Irregulars chatted and dined on Sherlock Holmes Beef, Moriarty Horseradish, and Baskerville Pudding. Presently they would ease back in their chairs for the rigid regularity of the after-dinner program. The aroma of pipe smoke would perfume the air and more than one of the assembled men would turn a head to see if it just might be possible to discover a tall slender figure lurking in a corner, the man for whom these rituals were celebrated.

"Well?" asked Wiggins. "What is your decision, Morgan?"

"Give me a little time, Wiggy."

"Time is running out."

"Until the end of tonight's dinner. I'll give you my decision this evening."

With an expression of complete dismay and disappointment Wiggins waddled away. Stopping to look at Morgan in the doorway, he said, "You surprise me, Morgan. I had expected to find a bit of Holmes in you. Sherlock would already be on the case."

"There is something to be said for prudence," said the tall man with the hawkish nose and piercing gray eyes as he came out of the shadows to stand beside Morgan.

"The whole proposition borders on the incredible. A bad piece of detective fiction."

"My dear fellow, life is infinitely stranger than anything which the mind of man could invent. If we could fly out of that window hand in hand, hover over this great city, gently remove the roofs, peep in at the queer things which are going on, the strange coincidences, the wonderful chain of events, working through generations, and leading to the most outrageous results, we would make all fiction with its conventionalities and foreseen conclusions most stale and unprofitable."

"Would you take this case if you could?"

"As a rule, when I have heard some slight indication of the course of events I am able to guide myself by the thousands of other similar cases which occur to my memory. I choose to be only associated with those

crimes which present some difficulty in their solution."

"Surely this one qualifies on that score."

"We do not have an abundance of facts at this moment. To let the brain work without sufficient material is like racing an engine. It racks itself to pieces."

"I suppose I owe something to my friends. Especially to Wiggins."

"A client is a mere unit to me. A factor in a problem. The emotional qualities are antagonistic to clear reasoning. If you take on this little problem, do it because of the interesting aspects of the case, not because of your emotional entanglements with the personalities concerned."

"This problem rightfully belongs with the police. I'm out of practice when it comes to homicide. I've become a specialist in the little things."

"To a great mind, nothing is little."

"I never claimed to be a great mind."

"Really, Morgan. Your modesty offends me. I cannot agree with those who rank modesty among the virtues. To a logician all things should be seen exactly as they are, and to underestimate oneself is as much a departure from the truth as to exaggerate one's own powers. I have been beaten four times—three times by men and once by a woman."

"But this case seems on the surface to be as bizzare as any you ever undertook."

"As a rule, the more bizarre a case is, the less mysterious it proves to be. You know my methods."

"I'm inclined to think—"

"I should do so were I you."

With clockwork regularity the Irregulars had proceeded in their rituals to the reading of the Constitution and By-laws. The recitation had fallen on the enormous shoulders of B. Alexander Wiggins as Morgan returned to his place at table Number One. "Four," said Wiggins. "All other business shall be left for the monthly meeting." Wiggins paused. "Five!" The room exploded with a chorus of Irregulars. *"There shall be no monthly meeting!"* To applause, Wiggins resumed his seat next to Morgan. "Well, are you for the game, Morgan?"

"Yes."

"Good show, Morgan. Good show."

8

The Observance of Trifles

It was raining as Morgan came out of the Queen Victoria Hotel. He wished he'd worn his deerstalker. Getting a cab would be impossible. Hundreds of Irregulars who had had the sense to wear their hats were swarming everywhere, some with umbrellas, all waving frantically for taxis, and none observing the rule about finding a safe one. Beneath the canopy of the hotel, conscious of a dour portrait of Victoria Regina glaring at his back, Morgan made up his mind to walk. He hoped the rain would turn to snow.

Somehow, snow seemed more acceptable than rain for walking, although it ended up by making a person just as wet. As Morgan was about to step out into the cold drizzle, Wiggins caught up with him. "I've given them the bad news about Herm Sloan and the good news about you coming to London with us. To a man, they are delighted and relieved. We're all going into the bar for a drink while this incredible crush for taxis clears up. Will you join us?"

Morgan shook his head. "I don't care much for wakes, which is what it'll be."

Wiggins shrugged. "I'll pick you up at five at your apartment." He clapped Morgan on the shoulder. "The game's afoot, old friend."

It was said with such jollity that Morgan experienced a fleeting sensation of being the butt of a joke. Only the hard reality of the death of Herman Sloan kept him from dismissing Wiggins, the Men of Tor, and their curious filing-card messages as a gigantic hoax. "Madness," he muttered as he stepped into the rain.

Immediately he thought about going to England. There would be, he assumed, rain in London, but he had noticed a difference between rain in London and rain in New York. There, it seemed more natural and pleasant than in New York City. He supposed it was because London was still primarily a city of low buildings and numerous small parks and squares, which softened the hard edges of inclement weather; in New York City the rain came down the tall canyons of skyscrapers with unrelenting hardness. Walking, Morgan began to look forward to seeing London again, to visiting old haunts, to strolling up Baker Street, to having a drink at the Sherlock Holmes Pub, and to renewing a friendship with Ivor Griffith of Scotland Yard.

At the corner of Park Avenue and Fifty-seventh Street Morgan hesitated. Three blocks east was Nicky's apartment house. Undecided, he hovered on the corner as the rain came down harder. A cab slowed and the driver peered through a streaky windshield. God, thought Morgan, a taxi driver is actually looking to see if he's got a fare on a rainy night in New York. Such miracles ought to be seized, he thought, but he wiggled a hand to dismiss the driver and the cab shot across Fifty-seventh Street. Morgan walked east.

From the corner of Second Avenue and Fifty-seventh he could look up nineteen floors of Nicky's apartment building and see her windows. Lights blazed in every one. Running, Morgan dodged traffic and skipped across vast seas of puddles to the lobby of the building. The familiar doorman smiled and touched the visor of his cap in greeting. "Is the lady in?" Morgan asked.

"She is, Mr. Morgan," replied the elderly doorman. "But she left word for me to tell you that she isn't. Sorry, sir."

Morgan jammed wet hands into his overcoat pockets. "Well, if she asks, Freddy, will you tell her that I *didn't* come around?"

The doorman chuckled. "I will, Mr. Morgan."

"What would New Yorkers do without their doormen, eh, Freddy?" he said, turning away. At the corner he waited half an hour for a downtown bus.

Sherlock Holmes peered impassively from Morgan's wall when Morgan sat down to telephone Kenny West.

His young associate seemed out of breath and agitated. "I have to see you in the morning, Kenny. Ten o'clock. Got a couple of chores for you."

"I'll be there," Kenny panted.

Morgan knew better than to ask Kenny what was going on. It being a Friday night, Morgan had a good idea what Kenny was up to. With his hands on the telephone he considered calling Ivor Griffith in London until he realized that in London it was already Saturday morning, and early at that. The rain against the windows was a torrent, now. Rain slashing against windows always made him feel warm and safe. Such a night was meant for reading, he thought, running his eyes along his shelves of books concerning Sherlock Holmes, but instead of taking down one of the books he reached for a shelf where he had a collection of video tapes of Sherlock Holmes films. Deciding was always a problem but he chose *Pursuit to Algiers* and watched it to the end of the scene where Nigel Bruce sang "Loch Lomond." Then he went to bed and slept until nine o'clock. He ate breakfast in a coffee shop across from his apartment house then walked uptown to his office on Lexington Avenue.

As soon as he opened the door of his office and looked across the room into Kenny West's face Morgan feared he was in for it. The youth was propped against the yellow oak desk with his arms folded across his chest and his legs planted apart as if ready to propel the lean and lithe body into violent action. Although he was leaning and apparently at ease there was in the flinty gray eyes, the set jaw, the tensed muscles of shoulders and thighs an impression of coiled tension. Kenny watched and waited without a word as Morgan closed the door and carried a blue garment bag bearing the name of Mel's Formal Wear to a clothes tree. Morgan hung the bag containing his rented tux on a hook, turned, glanced warily at his associate and went behind the desk. Kenny did not turn. "I'm sorry to bring you in on a Saturday, Kenny," Morgan said to Kenny's broad back.

"It was my Friday night that you screwed up."

Morgan dropped into his swivel chair. "Ah, when the phone rang you were . . ."

Kenny stood straight and turned slowly. "I was making love to the hottest number it has been my good fortune to meet in many a moon."

"Why'd you answer the phone?"

Kenny drifted from the desk and into the corner of a worn leather couch. "That's what she wanted to know."

Morgan cracked a grin. "What did you tell her?"

"I told her not to move."

"Did she?"

Kenny smiled. "The logistics would have been a little difficult." He sighed and stretched, extending his arms and linking his fingers. His knuckles popped like firecrackers. "It's crazy, I know, but there's a special sound to my phone when you call up. The bell seems louder. More urgent. Why the hell is that? How do you do it?"

Morgan lifted his feet to the corner of his desk. "I'm sorry I interrupted your calisthentics, Kenny. But I'd've kept calling every five minutes anyway."

Kenny shrugged. "It's okay. I made it up to her. Now, what is it, exactly, that needs to be done on a Saturday?"

Morgan flung his feet to the floor and leaned across his desk. "There's a pile of stuff. Some of it you can do

on the phone. There'll be a little legwork and you're
going to have to go out to Long Island, probably. Maybe
even to Boston. I'd handle some of it myself but I'm
leaving for London at seven o'clock. We've got ourselves a murder investigation."

Kenny's face lit up. "No shit?"

"Just like in the movies."

"Who got iced?"

Morgan winced. "A very nice old gentleman."

"Aren't the cops investigating?"

"Yes, but from their point of view it looks like the
tragic result of target practice. That's the Long Island
angle." He stared at Kenny for a moment then said,
"This is going to sound bizzare in the extreme, but hold
your questions until I give you the whole ball of wax."
Dutifully, intently, Kenny West listened to Morgan's
recitation of the events which had brought them to the
office on a cold gray Saturday morning in January.
When he was finished, Morgan cocked back in his chair
once more and cradled the back of his head in his
palms. "Whatcha think, kid?"

"I think you ought to stop hanging around with that
bunch of whackos."

Morgan smiled. "I am one of those whackos."

"I'm to go to Merrick and check on the shooting of
Mr. Sloan. You want me to find out the whereabouts of
Mr. Bell. I'm to check the veracity of all the little tales
your weirdo Holmes freaks dished out. The feuds, the
in-fighting, the blood-oaths, the quietly smouldering
vendettas."

" 'The observance of trifles,' in the words of the greatest sleuth of all time. That's your assignment."

Kenny rested his head against the back of the couch

and stared at the ceiling. "What's your theory?" He lowered his head and stared at Morgan from the tops of his eyes. "Who's really dealing out the cards?"

Morgan shook his head. "Between you and me, Kenny, a lot of the stuff Sherlock Holmes spouted off to Watson about the detection of crime was horseshit, but Holmes uttered one great truth that is the cornerstone of policework. 'It is a capital mistake to theorize before you have all the evidence.'" He pointed at Kenny. "That's why you're working on a Saturday and I'm flying to London tonight. I'll be at the Durrants Hotel. I'll call you or the answering service when I'm ensconced. You can call me when you've accumulated your assortment of trifles."

Kenny scratched his head. "Most of this is a little on the farfetched side. This Bell character. Nursing a grudge all these years? Why decide to get even now?"

"A very good question, Kenneth."

"And why the hell would someone with the reputation of Hess-Feldstein turn to murder when he can kill these characters with words everytime they write a new book? The TV guy might have a pretty good motive."

"If, in fact, he was scuttled by Ethan Remarque. There seem to be plenty of plausible reasons for a TV show to go down the drain long before it winds up on the tube. Still, it'd be nice to know where Leslie Westin is these days."

"I don't see any compelling reasons for murder in any of this, frankly."

"When has murder ever been reasonable?"

"What's on your agenda while I'm traipsing around the countryside?"

"When you find yourself heading for London on a couple of hours notice there are lots of things to do. And you're not the only one in this office with woman troubles."

"The wondrous Nicole." Kenny grinned.

"The wonder is that the cops aren't investigating my murder this morning. I'll speak with you from the Sceptered Isle, Kenny."

On the way out, Morgan picked up the blue garment bag to return to Mel's. Half an hour later, the doorman at Nicole Varney's address informed him Miss Varney was not in. At five o'clock B. Alexander Wiggins arrived with a limousine for the drive to the airport.

Baker Street

9
Flight to Baker Street

Slate-gray clouds had lowered. A cold mist turned to sleet. "The weather cooperates by setting a proper mood. How disappointing it would have been to depart for Baker Street under clear blue skies with a sparkling sun." Wiggins glanced at Morgan and smiled. "You've turned loose that young man, I presume."

Morgan nodded. "Kenny's on the case."

Wiggins sighed. "I wish I had had your foresight when I was a young man and had become a detective instead of an intellectual."

"Thanks for the compliment," Morgan said.

Wiggins smiled. "What is the indomitable Kenny's first assignment?"

"He's got half a dozen first assignments. There's Bell. There's the shooting of Herman Sloan. And so on."

"The solution lies in London," said Wiggins, turning his head toward the window of the limousine as it glided toward the Pan American Airlines terminal.

First class travelers may wait in Pan Am's starkly modern lounge with its own bar, comfortable chairs grouped around convenient tables, and if the travelers are not users of alcohol, free coffee in limitless quantities. Wiggins knew the way. Inside the lounge, the Men of Tor presented a morose picture huddled together in a corner. Unlike other passengers who were animated in conversation with silvery laughter punctuating their talk, the Men of Tor spoke little and then only in whispers. The death of Herman Sloan had cast a pall.

Carrie Lonsback of the Lonsback Travel Agency had been unable to break through the gloom. The arrival of Wiggins, whom she had found to be an amusing if somewhat bizarre personality, brought her to her feet and to his side. "We're not exactly off on a happy note," she announced. Then she turned to Morgan. "You're the last-minute addition to the passenger manifesto, I presume."

"David Morgan," he said with a smile.

"Carrie Lonsback," she replied, extended a hand.

"Charmed," he said.

"Charmed?" She shook her head. "The one characteristic of you Sherlock Holmes fellows that has always beguiled me is your quaint use of the English language. No one's ever told me that he was charmed by meeting me."

"But I am charmed," said Morgan.

"Well, come and join our glum little group," she said, turning away.

"A very pretty lady," whispered Morgan to Wiggins. His eyes followed Carrie Lonsback, a trim blonde moving through the first class passengers and the tables and chairs with the self-assurance of a person who knows her way around airport lounges and the people who use them.

"She does not know the true reason for your joining us," whispered Wiggins as they followed Carrie Lonsback toward the cluster of Men of Tor. "I explained that you are another Sherlockian interested in Sir Malcolm's project. I thought it would be unwise to let her in on our little mystery at this time. She might panic and cancel the trip. Once we arrive in London you may want to tell her everything. I leave that decision to you. She is a very attractive woman and I hope you won't let your attention stray from our purpose. This is an *affaire du crime* not an *affaire du coeur.*"

As the Boeing 747 found a smooth course above the weather and pointed itself toward England, Morgan struck up a conversation with Carrie Lonsback, taking her attention away from a pile of travel brochures laid out on the fold-down table in front of her seat. Wiggins caught Morgan's eye and made a face that suggested Wiggins expected better of the detective he had just engaged to work on a puzzling case. "To bend a cliché a bit," said Morgan to Carrie Lonsback, "what's a nice girl like you doing mixed up with a gang of Sherlockians?"

"The business of a travel agent, Mr. Morgan, is the travel business."

"You're not a Sherlockian, then?"

"It's a terrible thing to admit, but I've never read the stories. Travel's my passion. You and your friends are the Holmes experts. I suppose I ought to read up, though."

"I'll lend you a copy."

"Now you're teasing."

"Yes. But I do have several copies of the Holmes stories, as you might imagine." He smiled. "As a matter of fact I have about a hundred versions."

"A hundred?"

"Well, my Holmes books—ones about him and about his era plus the stories themselves—amount to a couple of hundred. It's a kind of lunacy, I suppose. You've met Sir Malcolm. His whole house is a Sherlock Holmes museum, I hear.

"Baskerville Hall. A big gloomy old English country house. Have you been there?"

"No. However, it's a legend among Sherlockians."

"You'll love it. Of course, it's not the Baskerville Hall in the story, is it?

"Baskerville Hall never existed. Sir Malcolm changed the name of the place when he bought it. Insanity. We're all crazy. You ought to be careful whenever you're in the company of Sherlockians. People might assume you're crazy, too."

"What is it about Holmes? What's the appeal?"

"Ah, volumes have been written on that subject. I like to think of it as a nostalgic yearning for a more civilized time. Sherlockians are stuck in the past. For example, you are in the travel business, and if someone were to ask you to name the most famous streets in the world you'd probably come up with a list that includes the Champs-Elysées in Paris, Broadway at night, the Street of David in Jerusalem, maybe Well Road in Shanghai. Ask a Sherlockian and the list will always begin with Baker Street." Amused and warming to the subject and noticing, happily, that Carrie Lonsback was interested, he went on. "Now, think of the most famous street *addresses* in the world. Number 10 Downing Street comes to mind, correct?"

"And 1600 Pennsylvania Avenue."

"*And* 221–B Baker Street. Interesting, isn't it? And

amazing that an address that never existed is one of the best-known addresses in the world. You can get into heated debates over the spot Conan Doyle had in mind for 221–B."

"And what is your choice?"

She was smiling and perhaps teasing him. "If you really want to know I'll take you there."

"Of course I want to know."

"It's a radical theory, I warn you. Sir Malcolm would throw me out of Baskerville Hall if I were to mention it in his presence."

"It will be our secret." She chuckled.

"That's enough of Holmes. The subject now up for discussion is Lonsback. I want to know everything."

"Not much to tell. Small-town girl attends snooty girls' school in New York, tries a fling at the publishing business, edits a travel book, falls in love with traveling and opens her own agency. It's been a struggle. There are plenty of travel agencies, as you may have noticed. I've tried to find a new twist. When I met Sir Malcolm Bannister the idea of the Sherlock Holmes tours was born."

"How'd you meet Sir Malcolm?"

"A chance encounter a year ago while I was in London. We were staying at the same hotel, the Durrants, where we'll be staying on this trip. It's Sir Malcolm's favorite hotel when he visits London. He was there while I was investigating the hotel to see if I ought to recommend it."

"Obviously you decided that you would recommend it."

"Oh, yes. You'll fall in love with it. First of all, it's only

3C

a few paces away from Baker Street. There's a Victorian atmosphere and the neighborhood is quiet. It's become one of my favorite hotels in London."

"Then you'll be staying at the Durrants with all the crazy Sherlockians on this airplane?"

"Naturally. And I'll be going to Baskerville Hall with you. We've got a full itinerary."

"I hope there's a little time left for a nice dinner somewhere quiet and completely removed from anything having to do with Sherlock Holmes."

"That's surprising. I'd've thought you would want to immerse yourself in Holmes every moment of the visit."

"That *was* my plan. Until I met you."

"Oh, you are dangerous, Mr. Morgan."

10

At Durrants Hotel

At dawn, like a parade of shining black beetles, four London taxis carried Morgan, Carrie Lonsback, and the Men of Tor from Heathrow Airport on the M4 highway to city routes that put the travelers onto Marylebone Road, Marylebone High Street, and George Street where they drew up in front of the white-columned entrance to Durrants

Hotel. Young bellmen in royal blue uniforms rushed to
gather their luggage and carry it into the lobby. Carrie
Lonsback paused in her duties of seeing that the registration process proceeded smoothly to touch Morgan's
sleeve. "Was I right? Do you love this hotel?"

Morgan surveyed the lobby. The Men of Tor stood at
the registration desk to his left. Beyond was the hall
porter's room where the bellmen picked up keys to the
rooms from pigeon holes before turning to the task of
collecting the baggage and the guests who belonged to
it. To the right of the lobby was a restaurant and ahead
of Morgan was a red-carpeted stairway rising to a landing from which the stairs branched right and left, but
the bellmen with their bags and their guests left the
lobby through a corridor leading to the lift, a writing
room, a bar, and the stairs down to the Edward VII
Breakfast Room.

Before following a bellman down the corridor, Ethan
Cage Remarque whispered to Morgan, "Must see you.
It's quite important."

"Speak to me now, Ethan."

"No," said the old man, scurrying away. "Later. I'll
come to your room."

"Number 228," said a bellman as he stood aside to
allow Morgan off the lift. "It's around in the back but
there's a shortcut through the fire stairway. It will save
you quite a few steps, sir. There's an ice dispens-
ing machine in there if you feel the need for a cold
drink."

"Can you fetch me a bottle of Scotch?"

"Easily done, sir."

The room was tucked in a corner with windows looking onto a courtyard. The room had twin beds, a large wardrobe, a small desk, a television set, and two chairs. The bathroom, he discovered with pleasure, had a large tub. Satisfied with the accommodations, he unpacked the suitcase containing articles he would need immediately for bathing and shaving. Then he picked up the telephone and placed a collect call to his answering service in New York. The night operator, a sexy voice named Evie, had a message from Kenny West. "He says the Merrick police are proceeding on the basis of the shooting having been an accident. Second, he says that the critic is out of town, possibly in Europe. Third, he's gone to Boston to follow the Bell angle. That's the lot, Mr. Morgan. Say hello to the Queen of England for me, and if you see that good-looking prince, the unmarried one, give him my number."

Morgan laughed as he hung up. He leaned back. A few moments later he was asleep. Two hours later he was awakened by the telephone. "If you've overcome your jet lag," said Carrie Lonsback without preliminaries, "how about joining me in the restaurant for lunch?"

Morgan struggled up. "Hell, what time is it?"

"A couple of minutes after noon."

"Christ, I just conked out on the bed."

"You and the rest of the boys. You fellows aren't very sturdy travelers if one little overnight flight can knock you out. I'm lonely down here. And famished. Which would you rather do? Sleep or eat?"

"I'll be down in a couple of minutes."

Hanging up the phone he realized that Ethan Cage

Remarque had not come around to his room as promised. For an instant he considered telephoning the
old man's room but gave up the idea. Entering the
bathroom to shave, he supposed the old man had fallen
asleep, too. Then he turned his thoughts to Carrie Lonsback and the happy idea of having lunch with her without the Men of Tor to keep them company. He found
her perched primly in a highback chair in the lobby.
"Hello, sleepyhead." She smiled. Standing, she said,
"You look almost human. Don't you just hate airplane
travel? I tried to persuade your Sherlockian friends to
make this journey on the *QE 2*. Steamships are so much
more civilized than jet planes, don't you think?"

Morgan took her arm. "Any woman who thinks like
that has the makings of a Sherlockian herself." A fleeting memory of Nicole Varney persuaded him not to
mention the Irregulars' rule concerning women.

By the time they finished eating, none of the Men of
Tor had put in an appearance. "We probably won't see
them until tea time," she said. "Then this evening
they'll be wide awake and unable to sleep. Tomorrow
they'll be more accustomed to being five hours ahead
in time. That leaves us the afternoon to ourselves, if
that's of any interest to you. What would you like to
do?"

"Need you ask when I'm so close to the most famous
address in all of literature?"

"To Baker Street?"

"If we're lucky, Holmes will be in."

Laughing, they stepped out of Durrants Hotel into a
clouded and chilly afternoon, swung right, and walked
west.

11
In Search of 221-B

When they turned onto Baker Street and Morgan hesitated, Carrie Lonsback asked, "Is one expected to genuflect?"

Morgan winced. "I warned you about Sherlockians."

"That was a cheap crack. I'm sorry."

"It is ridiculous. Here we have a street whose only fame is in fictional stories written decades ago yet to crazy people like me this place is Mecca, the Vatican, and Jerusalem rolled into one. Every time I come here it's the same feeling. The last time was eight or nine years ago. I was on a case and—"

"On a case?"

"You'll have to answer her question, Morgan."

"I've put my foot in it, haven't I?"

"Quite."

"I suppose I'll have to let her in on everything?"

"It is always awkward doing business with an alias."

"I'm a private detective, Carrie. I should have told you in New York. We all should have told you. I'm on a case. The Men of Tor have gotten threatening letters and—"

"My God, from whom?"

"They were anonymous. At first I was convinced they
were someone's idea of a prank. Until . . ."

"The death of Mr. Sloan?"

"There was also an attack on Wiggins."

"God. When?"

"Friday night. It may have been nothing more than
a mugging but there's the grim coincidence of it happening on the same day that Sloan was shot. The police
say Sloan was the victim of an accident. Perhaps. But
there is a possibility that someone is determined to
murder the Men of Tor."

"What are the police doing?"

"What would you do if you were a cop and I came to
you with this story?"

"I'd give you the bum's rush."

"If there is someone behind the attacks on Wiggins
and Sloan, then he means to go after the others. In that
case, he's likely to be here in London. Any chance of
stopping him lies here."

"So you came along as a bodyguard."

"My associate back in New York is following a few
leads, checking out possible suspects. He's young but a
very fine investigator and I'm counting on him to come
up with the origin of what could be death threats."

"What if he proves that the threats aren't a hoax?"

"I'll do my best to keep anything from happening to
the others while I turn the evidence over to the police.
I'm sorry if this puts a damper on your plans."

"The hell with me. David, if those men are in danger
you ought to be at the hotel with them."

"They're tucked snugly in their rooms. Any chance
I have of stopping the person behind this—if there is
one, and I'm not convinced that there is—is to play the

game loosely. Give him enough rope, as the saying goes. That's why we agreed to go ahead with this little business-cum-pleasure trip as planned."

"I'm glad you told me, David."

"I didn't intend to. But I'm glad I did, too." He smiled. "Anyway, it probably is just a Sherlockian's idea of a joke which just happened to coincide with an accident involving Sloan and a common mugging that chanced to include Wiggins."

"He is a character. Brilliant. *The* expert on Sherlock Holmes, I understand."

"Keeper of the flame."

"It must be quite a responsibility for him."

Morgan chuckled. "Wiggy regards it that way. With him, Holmes is more than an amusing hobby. I said I had a theory about the true location of 221-B. If you'd like to see . . ."

"Certainly. Lead on."

Morgan took her off Baker Street into Blandford Street and then into a mews named Kendall Place. He pointed to a four-story brick building with white-trimmed windows. "I believe this was the empty house in the story of that name. In the adventure, Holmes notices a window which had been closed for a long time in the empty house opposite his rooms on Baker Street. First it was closed. Suddenly it was open. Anything like that would make Holmes wonder, so he and Watson investigated. While they were sneaking toward the house by a long and circuitous route leading to the rear of the house, Mrs. Hudson was busy in Holmes's room with a wax effigy of Holmes. Its shadow on a drawn shade created a silhouette that looked exactly like Holmes. So, picture it: Mrs. Hudson is on her hands and knees every few minutes or so moving the dummy to make it look as if Holmes is at home and pacing the floor. Holmes is creeping up the stairs of the empty house with the trusty Watson at his side. Upstairs they pounced upon none other than Colonel Sebastian Moran, the right-hand man of the infamous Professor James Moriarty. Moran was there to kill Holmes. He got off one shot. Right through Mrs. Hudson's window and smack in the middle of the forehead of the wax dummy. Exciting stuff, hunh?" Carrie Lonsback nodded. Morgan grinned. Then they both laughed. "Anyway, I say that 221–B had to be just over there on Baker Street. Other Sherlockians disagree. And Sir Malcolm Bannister is adamant about this not being the spot. I'm sure I'm right, though."

"You love it, don't you, David?"

Surprised and embarrassed and with a sudden huskiness in his voice, Morgan muttered, "You bet I do." He cleared his throat and shrugged his shoulders as if the gesture could shake off his emotion. "Just up the street is the present address of 221 Baker Street. If you'd care to see it."

"Lead on, Mr. Holmes," she said with a nod.

"In Victorian London," Morgan lectured as they strolled north, "Baker Street was a far different avenue from this wide bustling commercial street of modern London. The Baker Street seen from Holmes's windows was lined with brick-front houses with little windows and iron handrails and gas lights above their gleaming white doors. In the murky swirl of foggy days, Holmes and Watson eyed the street of the dun-colored houses and listened for the clop and rattle of hansoms on the wet cobblestones. Then came the sound of Mrs.

Hudson's doorbell. Or Billy the page-boy barged in to announce the arrival of a client. Or they heard the tread of Lestrade's big feet on the steps."

"How many steps?"

"Seventeen. Then it was down the stairs in a flash and out into Baker Street in search of a cab. Never the first, nor the second, but the third. The game was afoot."

They crossed busy Marylebone Road and Morgan took her into the Baker Street underground station to show her a pub named for Moriarty and the walls of the station decorated with ceramic tiles bearing the Holmes profile. North of Baker Street's intersection with Marylebone Road they stood across the road from a huge gray office building, the location of the Abbey National Company. "That's the present 221 Baker Street. They still get mail over there addressed to Holmes." He stared at the building for a moment then looked at her with a boyish smile. "Of course the real 221–B wasn't here. If you want to know where 221–B really is, you have to look up here." He tapped a finger against his head.

12

High Tea

By the time they returned to Durrants Hotel snowflakes were flitting like moths in yellow light from the lamps glowing on the white pillars flanking the doorway. Above, a spotlighted Union Jack snapped against the wind that knifed east from Baker Street. Immediately. Wiggins lumbered toward them across the small lobby. "Where have you two been?"

"Baker Street," replied Morgan.

"You gave me quite a scare disappearing like that." Wiggins shot a quizzical glance at Carrie Lonsback.

"Carrie knows the whole story, Wiggy."

"That's best, I suppose. I'm sorry, Miss Lonsback, for not confiding in you before this." Rubbing his hands together, he said, "We are gathered in the dining room for high tea. Will you join us?"

"As soon as I check for messages. Carrie, you go on in with Wiggy."

A young man with a sallow complexion surveyed the pigeon holes in the hall porter's alcove and presented Morgan with a slip of yellow note paper. "An overseas call, sir. Came about an hour ago. Most urgent, the fellow said. Asks that you return the call."

"Is there a telephone in the lobby?"

"Phone box to your right, Mr. Morgan. Just pick up and the operator will put your call through."

Kenny West answered on the first ring. He sounded tired but undaunted. "The cops on Long Island definitely regard the Sloan shooting as an accident, although they haven't come up with the guy who was apparently such a lousy target shooter. If Sloan was iced on purpose it'll be up to us to prove it, not the Merrick police. On the whereabouts of the newspaper guy with the hyphen between his names, I can confirm that he is in London. Staying at the May Fair Hotel. Left Friday night on British Airways." Kenny paused and Morgan heard the faint shuffling of papers as Kenny leafed through his little black notebook. "That TV producer happens to be in England as well. How's this for the spooky coincidence department? Leslie Westin was on your flight."

"What? Are you sure?"

"Yeah. Traveled tourist class." Kenny chuckled. "Maybe you were sitting right beside him and didn't know it."

"We were in first class."

"I shoulda figured that."

"But it's possible that someone did see him. One of the Men of Tor—Ethan Remarque—said he had something important to tell me as we were checking into the hotel. It could be that Ethan recognized Westin."

"You don't know?"

"Well, he's an old man and he's been sleeping all afternoon."

"That would be genuine *chutzpah* for this Westin character to be going around bumping off Baker Street Irregulars and then wing off to England on the same plane with his victims. The mind boggles."

"What better way to keep an eye on the quarry? What else have you dug up? What's the story on Joseph Bell?"

"I'm gonna have to go to Boston for that. I made a few calls to some pals on a couple of Boston newspapers but there's nothing in their files on anyone named Bell that fits the guy we're interested in. I'm leaving for Boston soon's I hang up with you."

"Unless you've got more you can hang up now."

"Anything from your end?"

"It's starting to snow and it's time for tea."

Kenny laughed. "That's a picture I'd love to see. Dave Morgan sipping tea and munching crumpets."

"Call me from Boston if you come up with anything, Kenneth."

Wiggins, Benjamin Artnikoff, James Donald Cape, Bill Miner, and Carrie Lonsback waited around a table in a corner of the narrow wood-paneled dining room. A silver tea service sparkled in the center of the table. It was surrounded by trays of scones, Madeira cake, biscuits, and Yorkshire ginger cake. Wiggins announced, "We're all here but Ethan and Cliff. He's gone up to fetch Ethan. The old dear must be quite done in. The Do Not Disturb sign was on his door all day."

"I think I'd better go up there," said Morgan.

"Oh, Cliff will rouse him. They'll both be down presently. Sit. Have your tea," Ben Artnikoff insisted, and reached to pour. "Relax, David." He smiled. "It's a pity that this most civilized of English customs never caught on in America. Milk or lemon, Miss Lonsback?"

"Neither, thank you."

Artnikoff made a disapproving face. "Very un-British, if I may say so."

"Holmes took one or the other, I presume," she replied. "Do we know which?"

James Donald Cape spoke up. "It's lamentable that there isn't a clue in the Sacred Writings on that crucial point. By an odd turn of events it appears that Holmes was generally off on a case in afternoons."

"Or sleeping." Bill Miner chuckled. "Like Ethan."

"One assumes," continued James Donald Cape, "that

Mrs. Hudson served a very complete tea and that
Holmes and Watson consumed it with great gusto.
They were English, after all, and totally Victorian."

"How do you take yours, Morgan?" asked Benjamin
Artnikoff, tea pot at the ready.

"I'd rather have coffee."

"What a crude colonial you are," Bill Miner said.
"You'll have to settle for a cuppa. Tea's all we have."

"Milk, then. And plenty of sugar."

"How did we ever let this fellow into the Irregulars?"
teased Benjamin Artnikoff.

Morgan took one sip of the tea and watched Wiggins
pile a plate with one of each of the tempting delicacies
heaped before him, but Morgan's attention was di-
verted by the appearance of Cliff Brownglass's short,
thick figure in the doorway. "Here's Cliff."

As the Men of Tor turned and Cliff Brownglass
crossed the dining room, they forgot their tea and
delicacies which a moment before had been the center
of their attention. By the time Cliff Brownglass reached
the table, the same question sprang to each of their
minds. It was Morgan who asked it. "Where's Ethan?"

Ashen and shaken, Cliff Brownglass replied, "He
didn't answer when I knocked. His door's locked."

"He's probably just a sound sleeper," Carrie Lonsback suggested. "Have the desk ring his phone."

"I rang him from my room. No answer."

Morgan shot to his feet. "I'd better go up there."

"We'll all go," said Benjamin Artnikoff.

"No, I'll go alone," insisted Morgan. "We can't go
dashing out of here in a pack."

"I don't like the look of it," muttered Ben Artnikoff.

"Take a bellman with you. Have him unlock the room."

"Let Morgan handle it," snapped Wiggins. "He's the professional."

Some professional, thought Morgan as he left the dining room. Crossing the lobby toward the hall porter's alcove, the frail voice of Ethan Cage Remarque echoed in his mind. "Must see you. It's quite important."

The hall porter drew the extra key to Ethan Remarque's room from its pigeon hole. "Is something wrong, sir?"

"I hope not," said Morgan, striding to the lift. "I hope not."

13

The Speckled Band

"**L**ooks like the old gent's sleeping, sir," whispered the sallow young bellman as he pushed open the door to the dark of Ethan Cage Remarque's third floor room. A slant of light from the corridor slashed across the bed where the old man lay on his back, a blanket draped across him, his head turned atop a white pillow. Around his brow was a yellow bandana with brown speckles.

"Christ," sighed Morgan.

"Sir?"

Morgan switched on the lights and crossed the room. He stood beside the bed. "Ethan?"

"Sir, is the old gent . . .?"

"I'm afraid so."

"Must'a been his heart."

Morgan shook his head. "No. It's murder."

"Murder? Oh, sir, that's not likely."

"I suggest you use the phone by the bed and place a call to the police. It's murder by poison."

The bellman crossed the room slowly, his eyes fixed on the body of the old man with the speckled yellow cloth around his head. Lifting the phone, he asked, "How do you know it was poison? Are you a doctor?"

"No."

"Then how . . . ?"

"The Adventure of the Speckled Band."

"Beg pardon?"

"Nothing. Make the call to the police, please."

14

Chief Superintendent

The leafless trees of Sloane Square seemed to have been dusted with powdered sugar but their snowy pristine Christmas-card quality was lost on Chief Superintendent Ivor Griffith as he negotiated turns off the King's Road and around the square to Sloane Street. By the time he stopped for the light at Knightsbridge and Brompton Road his irritation at the weather had given way to grumbling resentment at being summoned from his cozy house on Chelsea's Cheltenham Terrace to drive all the way to George Street just because David Morgan was involved in a murder. If it was a murder. The police sergeant who telephoned had had his doubts. "An elderly gentleman is dead, Chief Superintendent, but it appears on the face of it to have been from natural causes. Heart failure, most likely."

"Heart failure hell," said David Morgan faintly. Then, strongly and angrily, Morgan was on the phone. "Ivor? Believe me it's murder. Get yourself up here as soon as you can."

"I'm confident that the officers who are there can handle it quite nicely, Morgan."

"Ivor, this goes far beyond tonight's murder."

"Are you in London in a professional capacity, Morgan?"

"Hell, yes. Are you coming or not?"

"I'm coming."

"This is one you'll be able to put in the Yard's Black Museum, Ivor."

Hyde Park was white with the light snow but Park Lane's blacktop was glistening wetly. "Boisterous weather," Griffith growled. Then he smiled. Morgan and murder. "What a character," he muttered. Who but Morgan would have the audacity to ring up a chief superintendent of the Metropolitan Police in the midst of a snowstorm and demand that he come and investi-

gate personally? Scenes of crime on snowy nights were
the province of the lower ranks. Certainly a death in a
hotel room—and probably a natural death—was not
something for a chief superintendent who recently had
been seconded to be Staff Officer to Her Majesty's Chief
Inspector of Constabulary. "Bloody flatfoot stuff, that's
what this is," Griffith mumbled as he turned into Upper
Grosvenor Street. The American Embassy loomed on
his left as he approached Grosvenor Square. "Leave it
to a Yank to muck up a Sunday evening." He turned
north, now, on Duke Street. "I should kick Morgan's
arse and will if this turns out to have been a heart
attack." North of Wigmore Street he navigated through
a flurry of snow and around Manchester Square. Dead
ahead stood Durrants Hotel. The street in front of it was
littered with police vehicles. Morgan was leaning coat-
less against a pillar in the doorway. "This better be
good, Morgan!"

"I had to raise hell before your men would telephone
you. How are you, Ivor? Sorry about this."

"Why do you say it's murder when my men say it's
a coronary?"

"Not a coronary. Poison."

The lobby of the hotel was a sea of uniforms, the blue
of hotel bellmen and the blue of London bobbies. A
handful of wide-eyed, horrified guests huddled at the
top of the stairway. A tall young police officer stepped
forward. "The body is on the third floor, Chief Superintendent. I'll show you the way."

"In a minute, Constable. I'll speak to Mr. Morgan
first. Is there a private place?"

"There's a writing room just down the corridor, sir,"
said the policeman, pointing.

In the room, Morgan crossed to a window looking into George Street. Fine snow stung the glass. Griffith closed the door and lingered by it. A lean man of middle age whose curly black hair was tinged with gray at the temples, a Welshman by ancestry, he had the kind of face which Morgan had known in his own Welsh relatives—straight-nosed, square-jawed, ruddy-cheeked. "Now what the devil's going on, David?"

Morgan moved into a heavily upholstered Morris chair. "The autopsy will show that Ethan was poisoned."

"Ethan?"

"Ethan Cage Remarque. A very fine old gentleman who never harmed anyone in his life. I know he was killed with a poison because that's how Dr. Grimesby Roylott was killed in *The Adventure of the Speckled Band.*"

"Say that again?"

"You'll find that a speckled bandana is wrapped around Ethan Remarque's head. In *The Adventure of the Speckled Band* it was a swamp adder coiled around Dr. Grimesby Roylott's brow. Obviously the deadliest snake in India is not easy to come by in London, so the murderer of Ethan Remarque would have used a poisonous injection and a bandana to simulate the snake."

"I'll have a look at the body," said Griffith. "Then you and I will have a chat, Morgan."

Chief Superintendent Griffith did not go immediately into the room. He paused in the doorway for a moment and in that instant entertained numerous thoughts and impressions. His policeman's eye took in the whole room as it had taken in other scenes of crimes, seeking an overall view before plunging into the scrutiny of and search for telling details. Fleetingly his mind appreciated the methodology of modern police procedure—photography, the lifting of fingerprints, the identification and cataloging of bits and pieces of physical evidence. Another part of his mind longed for an era when a policeman's only tools were his own intelligence, memory, and reason.

Stepping into the room, Griffith spoke to a young man who appeared to Morgan to be Indian or Pakistani, a doctor—probably a medical examiner. "Your preliminary diagnosis?"

"*Not* a coronary." The young man rolled his *R*s. Chief Superintendent Griffith rolled his eyes toward Morgan, who smiled. "Death appears to have been the result of an injection." Griffith rolled his eyes back to the young man. "Only the lab can tell us what was injected and whether it was an accidental overdose of medication."

"Did you find any medication in the room?" Morgan asked.

The young man with the rolling *R*s turned quizzically to Morgan. "None so far."

"You won't find any," said Morgan.

Griffith put a hand on the medical examiner's shoulder. "There's a possibility of poison. Can you check that out first in the autopsy?"

"Certainly."

"Have you found a needle?" asked Morgan.

"No," said the man with the rolling *R*s.

"You won't."

Chief Superintendent Griffith strode toward the door. "It's time for a chat, Morgan."

"My room's one flight down."

15
The Subtle Trap

"**L**et's talk murder, Morgan."

Morgan poured Scotch over ice in tall water glasses from the bathroom. Griffith had made himself comfortable on one of the two beds, his head and shoulders propped up by a pile of pillows against the headboard, and his feet crossed at the ankles. Morgan sat at the small writing desk and turned sidesaddle toward the chief superintendent. "There have been two murders and one attempted murder. Each incident was patterned on a Sherlock Holmes story."

"So what we have, in your opinion, is a thread of murder, a study in scarlet, crossing the Atlantic, and aimed at—whom?"

"Seven members of the Baker Street Irregulars."

"Christ." Griffith laughed.

"You can make light of it now, Ivor, but you won't laugh when you get your medical report on the cause of Remarque's death. Then you'll see that this is, indeed, a scarlet thread across the Atlantic. It's likely that the murderer has a gripe against one of the Irregulars and is going to murder several as a ruse. Are you willing to listen to me?"

"You're buying the drinks."

"I was skeptical, too, at first," Morgan began. Griffith listened impassively and moved only to sip his Scotch or adjust the pillows on which he was reclining like a

child listening to a bedtime story. A horror tale, Morgan
thought. Truly a study in scarlet. Of the shooting of
Herman Sloan, he asked, "Who goes target shooting in
the middle of the winter and close to a heavily traveled
road, one that leads to a railway station?" He gazed at
Griffith and answered the question himself. "Someone
gunning for human game." Of the attack on Wiggins he
asked, "What common street thief would take on a man
who weighs three hundred pounds? And with sticks?"
Griffith gave no sign of answering the questions. "The
cards bearing the single threatening word were done
by the same hand and by someone with a thorough
knowledge of the adventures of Sherlock Holmes.
Throughout these incidents one feels the presence of a
true student of the Sacred Writings. Add to this literary
expertise a knowledge of poisons and hypodermic needles—"

"The verdict is not in on those points, Morgan."

"I'm not worried at all about the outcome of the
autopsy. Poison by injection. It has to be. The speckled
band, for crissakes."

Griffith sat up and placed his Scotch on the table
between the twin beds. Looking at Morgan, he held up
three fingers. "The litmus test in a murder investigation, Morgan, involves three elements. Motive, means,
and opportunity."

"The motive was given to us. On the cards. *Rache.*
Revenge for some slight or betrayal or perceived
wound God-knows-how-long-ago. Opportunity? All the
suspects I've named for you were in New York and are
now in London. I'm not sure about Bell. But he may be
here."

"Good of you to bring them with you, Morgan."
Griffith picked up and drained his glass. "And it was
damned cheeky of that television chap, Mr. Westin, to
fly on the plane that brought you and your friends to
London. But what about your more intimate traveling
companions? From what you've told me, most of them
have a motive of some kind, strong or weak, but a motive nonetheless. And they've all had the opportunity.
What about the means? How many of your Sherlockian
pals are conversant with the instruments of murder—
poison and the requisite needle? All of them? They're
mystery buffs. Is there one of them who has a better knowledge of hypodermic syringes than the
others?"

"God, yes. Cliff Brownglass. He's a diabetic. Carries
needles with him."

"And insulin's a potent killer if given in a strong dose.
And wasn't Mr. Brownglass the one who went looking
for Mr. Remarque? In Brownglass you have all three
elements, Morgan. Motive? The old man put the kibosh
on a TV deal that Brownglass was interested in. Means?
A diabetic's needle. Opportunity? Mr. Brownglass
came upstairs alone looking for the old man. I'd say that
Mr. Brownglass would be a prime suspect. *If* this were
a case of murder, which I'm not convinced of. The
elderly chap may have O.D.'d."

"Hell, Ivor, you surely don't believe that old man was
on drugs?"

"It's the new recreation."

"Where's the needle?"

"The boys haven't finished searching the room yet."

"They won't find a needle. The cause of death is

supposed to be a poisonous snake. The speckled band. The killer would sacrifice the effect if he left a syringe behind."

Griffith stood. "Are you describing a murderer or a theatrical director?"

"We're dealing with a very theatrical murderer, Ivor."

"We'll see. I'll have a look at the autopsy report. I'll wait until everything is analyzed. In the meantime, you and your friends ought to stay put. It's a request not an order. I'd feel better if you'd enjoy London a while longer before you go to Devonshire and Sir Malcolm's country estate."

Morgan shook his head. Pacing the room, he asked, "May I propose an alternative?"

Griffith sat again, a study in puzzled amusement. "I'm willing to listen."

"We've got to determine if the murderer—assume we are dealing with murder for a moment, please—if the murderer is Bell, Westin, Hess-Feldstein, or one of the Men of Tor."

"How do you propose that? By asking them?"

"I suggest you allow us to proceed with our visit to Sir Malcolm's."

Griffith toyed with the drained Scotch glass and shook the remnants of ice cubes at the bottom. "Now you want to turn this drama into Agatha Christie. A group of suspects and/or victims in the old English country house. What do you want me to do while you are plodding across the moors to Baskerville Hall?"

"Some of your detectives in the C.I.D. could keep a

discreet watch on Westin and Hess-Feldstein. If they go
about their business in London we know that our murderer is one of the Men of Tor. If either gets a yearning
for the clean air of Devonshire . . ."

"That's playing fast and loose with lives, Morgan.
There may, indeed, be a murderer in your jolly group.
You're asking me to step aside and give him a chance
to commit another murder."

"If we don't nab him here in England he'll be free to
act at will when we return home. Picking off his quarry
one at a time. But that's not what he wants. He wants
the thrill of murder while we are all together. We have
to play the game by his rules, Ivor, or we lose it. Let's
run out the skein a bit."

"The subtle trap, the clever forecast of coming
events?"

"Well put, Ivor."

"Yes. By your favorite sleuth in *The Valley of Fear.*"

Morgan grinned. "You're game for it?"

Chief Superintendent Griffith set aside his glass,
stood, and gathered up his hat and coat. "If there
weren't one of the best detectives in the business
going out to Devonshire with the Men of Tor I wouldn't
even consider it. Not for a second." He paused at the
door, hat in hand. "To give all this a little more credence, I'll inform your pals that they are not to leave
the city until I give the word. With appropriate solemnity I will advise them that they are all under suspicion
until I receive the report on the cause of Mr. Remarque's death. I'll hold you here for only a day. Some-
time tomorrow afternoon I'll inform you and the others
that the report from the medical examiner showed

death by natural causes. That will probably disappoint the murderer and make him think that the men of Scotland Yard are as obtuse as they were portrayed in the Sherlock Holmes stories—which was a slander that Conan Doyle should never have been permitted to perpetrate, by the way. It will also give the murderer a sense of security. I'll have time to set up a discreet surveillance of Westin and Hess-Feldstein. I would say that you'll be able to leave London just one day late for your visit to Sir Malcolm's dreary little house on Devonshire's Dartmoor. Of course, if he tries it again in London . . ."

"He won't."

"Why not?"

"Because he's having too much fun stretching out the suspense. Hell, if he'd wanted to get it over with in a hurry he could have blown up our airplane. I think the murderer will pause for effect. By the time he's ready to strike again we'll be at Baskerville Hall."

"Of course, there's the matter of explaining the speckled band."

"Christ, I'd forgotten about that."

"Except for you, my men, and the bellman, no one else knows of it. I'll make sure the existence of the devilish piece of cloth remains our secret. Cheerio, Morgan."

"Ivor?"

"Yes?"

"About Holmes's rather dim view of the fellows from Scotland Yard? Lestrade, especially. Belated apologies."

Chief Superintendent Griffith cracked a smile. "Well, Lestrade was a bit of dolt, wasn't he?"

16
The Dog in the Night-time

At three in the morning, Morgan got out of bed, dressed, packed one pipe, slipped a second into his pocket with his tobacco pouch, took the short-cut to the lift, strode down the silent corridor to the lobby, and turned toward the street. The night hall porter, an elderly man with a white military mustache, leaned from his alcove. "Everything all right, Mr. Morgan?"

"Everything's fine. Can't sleep, though."

"Understandable, sir, what with what happened."

"The others are all in their rooms?"

"They are indeed, sir."

"And the extra keys?"

The old man glanced at the pigeon holes. "All accounted for, sir. If you're going for a stroll, sir, be careful. Streets are not always safe this time of night."

"Thank you. I'll be alert." In the lamplight outside the entrance to the hotel Morgan paused to light his pipe.

"It's quite a three-pipe problem, Morgan."

"It surely is."

"May I walk with you?"

"It would be an honor."

"In the event that it would interest you, may I say that I approve of the scheme you've worked out with

Chief Superintendent Griffith? I have not always held the professionals of Scotland Yard in the highest esteem, as you know, but this Griffith fellow seems to be rather bright and promising. There may be an occasional want of imagination down at the Yard, but they lead the world for thoroughness and method."

"What do you make of these crimes?"

"Crime is common. Logic is rare. Therefore it is upon the logic rather than upon the crime that you should dwell. Until this moment I was convinced that the days of the great cases were past. I had begun to think that man, or at least criminal man, had lost all enterprise and originality. From the point of view of the criminal expert, London has become a singularly uninteresting city since the death of the late unlamented Professor Moriarty. The community is the gainer, and no one the loser, save the poor out-of-work specialist, whose occupation has gone. With that man in the field one morning's paper presented infinite possibilities."

"This adventure of the Men of Tor would be worthy of Moriarty if he were alive."

"I quite agree. It's the work of a complex mind. All great criminals have that. My old friend Charlie Peace was a violin virtuoso. Wainwright was no mean artist. It is fortunate for this community that I am not a criminal. They say that genius is an infinite capacity for taking pains."

"I must confess that at the moment I'm stymied."

"There is nothing more stimulating than a case where everything goes against you. You have a full roster of suspects."

"There's my old friend Wiggins."

"Yes. His is an interesting story. Of the three incidents concerning the Men of Tor, the attack on him is
singular in that the only evidence of it comes from
Wiggins. But, of course, you've made note of that
fact."

"The critic Hess-Feldstein, what do you make of
him?"

"For a newspaperman to turn to murder to avenge
an insult seems rather extreme. As I observed to Watson in *The Six Napoleons*, 'The Press is a most valuable
institution if you know how to use it.' Mr. Hess-Feldstein may be a poisoner, but the venom is at the tip of
his pen, I believe, and not in a hypodermic needle."

"And Mr. Leslie Westin?"

"I would say that a man whose chief occupation is
producing television programs has committed quite
enough crimes without adding genuine murder to the
list. Still, it is interesting that Mr. Westin traveled with
you—although you did not notice it at the time. If
criminals would always schedule their movements like
railway trains it would certainly be more convenient
for all of us."

"Everywhere I turn I find someone with powerful
motives for murder: revenge or profit. Or both."

"Yes, however, one should always look for a possible alternative and provide against it. It is the first rule
of criminal investigation. Wiggins has reason to resent
Benjamin Artnikoff. Artnikoff, himself, told you there
was no reason not to suspect him. Cliff Brownglass was
affected by Ethan Remarque's intervention in the business concerning Mr. Westin. All had reason to make

Mr. Hess-Feldstein angry perhaps to the point of murder. And there is the question of Mr. Joseph Bell. You know my methods."

"It is always dangerous to reason from insufficient data."

"Quite so."

"Beware of circumstantial evidence."

"True, but circumstantial evidence is occasionally very convincing, as when you find a trout in the milk. It is not really difficult to construct a series of inferences, each dependent upon its predecessor, and each simple in itself. If, after doing so, one simply knocks out all the central inferences and presents one's audience with the starting point and the conclusion, one may produce a startling effect, though possibly a meretricious one. Perhaps when a man has special knowledge and special powers like ours it rather encourages him to seek a complex explanation when a simpler one is at hand. How often have I said that when you have eliminated the impossible, whatever remains, however improbable, must be the truth? In solving a problem of this sort, the grand thing is to be able to reason backwards. That is a very useful accomplishment, and a very easy one, but people do not practice it much. In the everyday affairs of life it is more useful to reason forwards, and so the other comes to be neglected. There are fifty who can reason synthetically for one who can reason analytically. The world is full of obvious things which nobody by any chance ever observes."

"Such as the dog that did nothing in the nighttime."

"Precisely."

"Have you any other advice to give me in this three-pipe problem?"

"You have really done very well indeed. It is true that you have missed everything of importance, however."

17
Kippers and Red Herrings

Twenty minutes after he sat down for an English breakfast in the Edward VII room of Durrants Hotel, Morgan was joined by Carrie Lonsback. She did not notice him at first as she waited inside the door for a waiter to seat her. Morgan used the moment to study her and admire her. A white knitted sweater draped her shoulders. Her dress was a deep purple, almost black, as if she had chosen it for mourning. Her blond hair was swept up and made her look older, more austere. She clutched a small black leather purse in one hand and a large soft brown leather bag in the other. When she noticed him at his corner table she jerked her head in recognition and crossed the noisy room. "You're up early."

"Couldn't sleep."

"Neither could I. What a tragic thing. You talked with the police. Do they believe Mr. Remarque was murdered?"

Morgan hesitated, thinking. Then the lie sprang easily to his lips. "No. They're convinced it was a natural death."

"And what do you believe?"

"They're the experts. I'm not a homicide expert. Even when I was a cop I didn't handle many homicides. I can accept death by natural causes."

"But they've told us not to leave London."

Morgan shrugged. Finding that lying was easy, he said, "That's pretty much routine until the reports are in. In a couple of hours someone will call up from Scotland Yard and tell us we're free to do whatever we wish."

Frowning, reaching across the table to touch his hand, Carrie Lonsback asked, "Do you believe Ethan was murdered?"

"No, I don't."

"From all that you told me, and because of the man who died in New York—"

"That probably was an accident. And Ethan was an old man."

"I've been worrying about what we ought to do. It's unthinkable to go on as if nothing had happened. I'm going to suggest to the others that we call off the trip and return home."

"Don't do that. You'd only make them feel worse. Believe me, because I know these men. The best thing to do is continue with the visit to Sir Malcolm's as planned. And I think we ought to go out tonight to dinner—all of us—and, well, have a good time. Ethan was always for a good time. I think the best thing we could do in his memory would be to have dinner." He paused, smiling. "And why not at the Sherlock Holmes

Pub down on Northumberland Street? We'll get a table upstairs and drink a toast to one of the greatest Sherlockians of them all. Ethan would be pleased." Warming to the idea, he lifted her hand in his. "Have you ever been to the pub? It's marvelous. Upstairs in the restaurant they have a re-creation of Holmes's study at 221–B. It's wonderfully authentic and quite romantic. You sit beside a large window that separates the study from the restaurant and you get the distinct feeling that you're dining in Sherlock's digs. It'll be fun."

A waiter interrupted. "Would you care to order, miss?"

Startled and unsure, she picked up a menu. "I haven't looked."

"Oh, you must have the kippers, Carrie. You *are* in England, after all."

She smiled and nodded. "Kippers it'll be."

"For two, waiter."

A few minutes later, watching her eat the fish, he regretted having lied to her about the cause of Ethan Remarque's death.

"Never let emotion get in the way of your business, Morgan."

"You needn't come around preaching your methods, I know them. I've studied The Canon."

"You're one of those men who needs to confide in someone—preferrably a woman. There are times when it's best to hold your cards close to your chest."

"Would you deny me my Watson?"

"You'll recall that I sometimes withheld certain facts, certain decisions, certain paths of deduction

from Watson. Especially in the early stage of an investigation. There are instances when a solution is more
easily reached by an open discussion of the problem.
I do not think you are at that stage in this very interesting problem, Morgan. At the moment, confide in no
one. Allow no one to muddy the waters of your logic.
I would suggest that there are elements of this mystery
which you might withhold even from Chief Superintendent Griffith of Scotland Yard."

"Ivor Griffith is several cuts above the Lestrades
of your day."

"He is an official police officer. Therefore, he is
encumbered. The beauty of the private consulting detective, Morgan, is in his freedom of thought and action."

"Thank you very much. Now may I have my breakfast?"

"You seem distracted," said Carrie Lonsback.

Morgan shrugged off his thoughts and forced a smile.
"You've done your hair differently. I like it this way.
Gives you a no-nonsense look."

"Well, I—"

The vast shadow of B. Alexander Wiggins fell across
them. "Ah, here you are. Kippers! Capital idea. Waiter?
The same for me. A double order." Drawing a table
next to theirs, he sat, overflowing the small rattan chair,
and propping his leg-of-lamb arms upon the table. "So,
Morgan, are we all under suspicion by the boys from
the Yard?"

"The preliminary opinion is that Ethan died naturally."

"But of course you don't believe that?"

"I have no reason not to believe it." The lie slipped out easily. "Ethan was an old man."

"Poppycock. Ethan was fit as a fiddle. Did you look for a signature to the crime? An indication of which of the adventures was the pattern for the murder?"

"There were no signatures, Wiggy."

"You must have overlooked it. Ethan's death was not a natural one. To believe so is to stretch credulity."

"Must we dwell on it?" asked Carrie Lonsback.

"I'm sorry, my dear. I should have thought about how this must have affected you." Wiggins patted her hand. "I'm afraid we've done you a great disservice by bringing you with us under these circumstances. I . . . we . . . would understand if you packed your bags and went back to New York."

"Are you returning?" she asked.

Wiggins waved a hand to dismiss the question as the waiter laid before him his double order of kippers. "I will stay the course. I'll not be intimidated." Chewing, he looked up at Cliff Brownglass threading his way across the Edward VII room. "I'm certain Cliff is as determined as I to remain here in England, to continue to Baskerville Hall, and to transact the business which brought us across the water. Is that correct, Clifford?"

"Is what correct?"

"That the Men of Tor are committed to pushing ahead in spite of these murders."

Cliff Brownglass pulled out a chair. Sitting, he nodded. "Certainly we're staying. Was there any doubt?"

"Not on my part," said Wiggins, chewing.

Cliff Brownglass turned a jowly face to Morgan. "And you?"

"Count me in. I've never been to Baskerville Hall.

What true Sherlockian would turn down a chance to see it?"

"Besides," Wiggins said, "I'm his client and he stays on the case until I dismiss him or he solves it. We never did discuss a fee, Morgan. Are you going to charge me for your services?"

"He'll split the royalties on the book which I'm sure you'll write about this case." Cliff Brownglass, studied the menu through half-frame reading glasses and chuckled. "Be careful, however, Morgan, that Wiggy doesn't cut you out of the profits the way Ben Artnikoff cut him short. Wiggy pouted for months after that episode."

"Stuff and nonsense, as Ethan liked to say. Ben was perfectly correct in going ahead with the project without me. It had changed considerably from the original concept."

"Ben thinks you still nurse a grudge," said Morgan.

"Benjamin Artnikoff has a flair for exaggeration. That's the secret of his success as a writer."

"He even suggested that it was a motive for . . ."

"Murder?" Wiggins laughed. "Sweet Ben. What would we do without his rapier wit?"

Carrie Lonsback shuddered. "Why are we talking about murder if the police say Ethan died of natural causes?"

"Is that what they say?" asked Cliff Brownglass.

"That's the preliminary report," said Morgan.

"Bring me the kippers, too," said Cliff Brownglass to a waiter. Turning to Morgan, he asked, "Is that also your opinion?"

"There were no signs of violence in the room."

"The best murders are conspicuous by their lack of

signs of violence," said Wiggins. "Death can come with
the prick of a pin, the drop of poison in a glass of water
at the bedside, a trace of strychnine under the cap of
the toothpast tube. Why, a man may even be frightened to death."

"Stop it," snapped Carrie Lonsback.

Wiggins touched her hand again. "You must understand, my dear, that Cliff and I are—well, for want of
a better way of putting it—whistling through the grave-
yard. It's impossible for any of the Men of Tor not to talk
about these curious deaths. I'm sorry if it upsets you,
but there it is."

"Aren't you frightened at all?"

"No one confronts the possibility of imminent death
without at least a trace of apprehension. But there is
also, in this instance, an overriding sense of excitement.
Anticipation, even. Do you follow?"

"What you're saying is, you're enjoying this."

"Probably as much as the murderer," Wiggins said.

Benjamin Artnikoff appeared in the doorway, waved,
and came to the corner. "Is this a conference or a
wake?"

"Both," said Wiggins.

"We were discussing our immediate plans in view of
the unpleasantness of last evening," said Cliff Brownglass.

"We're all trying to keep a stiff upper lip," said Wiggins.

"Not thinking of quitting the field, I hope?" said Ben
Artnikoff as he sat beside Morgan.

"Perish the thought," Wiggins said. "I was trying to
explain to Miss Lonsback that, while we regret and
mourn the deaths of two of our Irregular fellows, we are

all caught up in this adventure and are determined to press on and damn the torpedoes."

"Yes, I agree that that's the picture, Miss Lonsback. We would understand if you chose to leave. However, I think everyone here will agree that you are in no danger yourself. Would you concur, Morgan?"

"Miss Lonsback is certainly in no danger. Frankly, I have grave doubts that anyone is in danger. The police in New York say Herm Sloan was shot accidentally. Wiggins was probably mugged. Scotland Yard says Ethan died naturally. All of our conjecture about threats and vendettas is just that—conjecture. I believe it would be foolish to call off the visit to Baskerville Hall on the basis of a string of coincidences and a joke played by someone with a warped sense of humor." He turned to Carrie Lonsback. "No one would blame you if you wanted to go home, but everyone would miss you."

"Especially you, Morgan." Wiggins chuckled.

"I certainly am not going to run away if you men are determined to stay," she said defiantly. "Were I to leave that would amount to a signal to the murderer—if there is one—that he had frightened me off. I'd disgrace my sex, wouldn't I?"

"Good girl," said Ben Artnikoff, slapping the table.

"Who knows? You might prove to be helpful to Morgan as he goes about his sleuthing," added Wiggins, his cobalt eyes twinkling in the slits of his puffy face. "And should Morgan and Scotland Yard prove correct, we will all go home with a wonderful excursion behind us and a handsome business deal transacted. There is something to be said for looking at the brighter side. And we do owe something to Herman and Ethan, don't we?"

"It's settled, then. We're off to Baskerville Hall," said Cliff Brownglass.

"As soon as the chief superintendent gives us leave," said Wiggins. "If he and his experts believe that Ethan died of natural causes, we should be on our way soon."

"We ought to put the question to Jimmy Cape and Bill Miner," said Morgan. "Where are they? Anybody see them this morning?"

"Don't get that worried-detective look, Morgan," said Wiggins. "Bill and Jimmy are in the reading room with the morning papers. Neither was especially hungry, apparently." Pushing aside his coffee cup, he went on, "Since Scotland Yard has delayed our departure for Baskerville Hall, what do you gentlemen propose we do to kill the day?"

"An unfortunate turn of phrase, Wiggy," muttered Ben Artnikoff.

"What about the British Museum?" asked Cliff Brownglass.

"Excellent idea," said Wiggins.

"We'll stay together," said Cliff Brownglass.

"The better to keep an eye on each other." Wiggins smiled.

"As for me," said Morgan, "I believe I'll have a look around London. The snow's stopped. Looks like a good day. Would anyone care to join me?"

"I will," said Carrie Lonsback happily.

"What about the Men of Tor?" he asked.

"Oh, there's not one of us who would care to stand in the way of two people who wish to stroll hand-in-hand through Berkeley Square," Wiggins said, expansively.

18
Victorian Streets

Morgan looked west to Baker Street. "Oh, we're not going that way again?" moaned Carrie Lonsback.

With a laugh, Morgan asked, "Which direction, then?"

"Anywhere but Baker Street. Let's put Sherlock Holmes completely out of our minds, at least for a while. How about a gentler literary figure?"

"Whom do you have in mind?"

"Elizabeth Barrett Browning. We're only a couple of blocks from Wimpole Street. I happen to have written a senior thesis on Elizabeth and Robert Browning. You have your Victorian idols, I have mine."

"The year's at the spring
And day's at the morn;
Morning's at seven;
The hillside's dew-pearled;
The lark's on the wing;
The snail's on the thorn:
God's in his heaven—
All's right with the world."

"A detective who recites Robert Browning's poetry. You're filled with surprises, Mr. Morgan."

"Isn't there a Browning couplet lurking in a corner of your mind? As long as we're being poetic."

"You, being a man, expect me to recite Elizabeth. Well, brace your male ego, Mr. Morgan. Here's my favorite bit of Browning. Robert, that is." She stepped away a pace and jammed her hands against her hips. "Ready?"

"Ready," he laughed.

> "Rats!
> They fought the dogs and killed the cats,
> And bit the babies in the cradles,
> And ate the cheeses out of vats,
> And licked the soup from the cooks'
> own ladles."

"Charming!"

She linked arms with him as they walked toward Marylebone High Street. "My father used to read that to us. *The Pied Piper of Hamlin.* I was quite a tomboy."

"Why do tomboys always grow up to be beautiful?"

"Do they?"

"You did."

"Yes, you are dangerous."

They turned onto New Cavendish Street heading toward Wimpole Street but Morgan stopped short. "Fantastic. Look at this. A train store. God, a block from the hotel. We must go in. Did I tell you I love trains? I've got an entire room in my apartment that's nothing but trains. A certain friend of mine castigates me for the extravagance. 'David,' she scolds, 'it is insanity to pay New York City rents for an extra room just to put up a toy train set.' Toys! Every time she says that I get furious. She also disparages my affection for Sherlock Holmes. I don't know why I put up with her."

"Why do you?"

Morgan shrugged and pushed open the door to the train store. Before going in, he turned to her. "You've got nothing against trains?"

"David! I'm a travel agent!"

Holmes vanquished the Brownings as they roamed the neighborhood east of Baker Street. "Harley Street," announced Morgan, turning his head left and right, "is the prestige avenue for London's medical profession. Up and down these blocks these impressive townhouses are crammed with the consulting rooms of physicians. Poor old Watson never could get an address here. Had to settle for offices 'round the corner. Things never did come together for Watson. Except in his friendship with Holmes, of course." Farther east he pointed to a building housing the British Broadcasting Corporation. "This was the Langham Hotel. It plays a role in *The Sign of the Four, A Scandal in Bohemia,* and *Lady Frances Carfax.*" A block from the Langham, turning west again, Morgan pointed down Wigmore Street. "Holmes trod these pavements often. He took in concerts at Wigmore Hall. The post office farther along this street was used by Holmes and Watson. In *The Sign of the Four,* Holmes knew Watson had been to the Wigmore post office because of red clay clinging to Watson's boot. There'd been road construction underway near the post office and the red clay they dug up was unique to this part of London." Presently, they turned north on Duke Street, ambled around Manchester

Square lined with gray-faced houses with their crisp
white pillars, and lazily walked the final block to
George Street.

One police car was parked in front of Durrants Hotel.
Beside it, Morgan recognized a young constable from
the previous evening. Touching the tip of his bobbie-
hat in a salute, he said, "Good afternoon, Mr. Morgan.
Afternoon, miss. Sir, the chief superintendent wonders
if you could come to his office?"

Morgan smiled. "Am I under arrest, Constable?"

"Hardly, sir," The constable chuckled. "The chief superintendent assures you that he won't require very
much of your time."

"I do have a dinner engagement."

"You'll be back in plenty of time, sir. I'll drive you
back myself."

19

New Scotland Yard

"**T**hey call it New Scotland
Yard," said the constable as he threaded the police car
through traffic and around the Queen Victoria Memorial in front of Buckingham Palace. "But to be accurate
you ought to call it *New* New Scotland Yard." He negotiated a turn onto Birdcage Walk and past Wellington
Barracks. "The original Scotland Yard was on the site of

an old palace used by the Scottish Kings when visiting London. That was the Yard where Lestrade and others worked in Sherlock Holmes's day."

"Ah, you're a student of the Sacred Writings?"

"Every English schoolboy reads Holmes, sir. When the Yard vacated the original premises it moved to the buildings near Number Ten Downing Street. You probably visited the Yard there, down the little hill known as Derby Gate? The wonderful yellow-brick buildings?"

"Yes, I remember."

"We call that Old Scotland Yard today but when the police first moved there in 1890 it was New Scotland Yard. Now our present headquarters is called New Scotland Yard, if you follow. As I say, we ought to call it *New* New Scotland Yard, eh? And here we are."

The highrise building of the Metropolitan Police paled in comparison to the yellow-brick, turreted structures of Victoria Embankment, Morgan thought as the constable escorted him into a spartan lobby and toward a bank of elevators. Chief Superintendent Ivor Griffith greeted them when they got off. "Morgan, thanks for coming. I thought I'd save time and bring you here straight away because I knew you'd want to see the reports of our laboratories yourself."

"You've got the verdict on Ethan Remarque?"

"We have," said Chief Superintendent Griffith, pushing through swinging doors into a vast laboratory gleaming under fluorescent lamps and scented faintly with chemicals. "His death was as you suggested."

"Poison."

"Thorazin. Are you familiar with it?"

"A powerful sedative."

"Exactly. There was enough of it in Mr. Remarque to kill him and half the Queen's Horse Guards. The report and the other findings of our examination of the room are on a desk in the corner. You'll want to look them over, I assume?"

"I would," said Morgan, drawing out a chair at a desk, bare except for a small pile of folders.

"Your murderer knows his way around with syringes," said Chief Superintendent Griffith, sitting on the corner of the desk.

Morgan opened the first folder. "How the hell do you get someone to lie there while you shoot Thorazin into him?"

"The answer's in the second folder. There were cotton fibers deep in the nostrils and mouth, indicating that a pillow was held against the old man's face. He was held down, his cries muffled by the pillow, while the Thorazin was administered. It took quite a bit of dexterity to hold him with one hand and inject the drug with the other."

"Maybe the killer had help."

"Folder three. The lab boys are reasonably certain one man did it. It's all there in technical jargon if you care to read it."

"I'll take your word for it."

"Jolly good of you."

Morgan closed the folders. "It doesn't look good for Cliff Brownglass, hunh?"

"He's diabetic. Knows needles. Big fellow. Strong."

Morgan shook his head. "It's too obvious, Ivor."

"There's more than enough cause to pick him up."

"Don't."

"Morgan, you are incredible. The evidence is there. I have an obligation to have him questioned."

"Stick with our plan, Ivor."

"I oughtn't be involved at all. I'm not in the Yard anymore. I'm seconded to the Home Secretary. If I continue to interfere with a criminal investigation there'll be bloody hell to pay."

"And there'll be bloody hell to pay if you arrest Cliff and there's another murder committed."

"And what if Clifford Brownglass is the murderer?"

"Stick to the plan we agreed on, Ivor. Stop being a goddamned stuffy bureaucrat and be the cop you trained all your life to be."

Chief Superintendent Griffith looked away from Morgan and out the window of the laboratory. Above the bare treetops of St. James's Park he saw the roof of Buckingham Palace and behind it the lowering gray skies of a London January afternoon. "You want me to let you and your bizarre friends go to Devonshire, knowing damned well there's a killer in your midst."

"We don't know that for certain. There's still Westin. Hess-Feldstein."

"It's a quick way for me to be cashiered, Morgan."

"You can sell your memoirs. Get a big Hollywood deal. Move to Los Angeles."

"We're playing games with lives, Morgan."

"We'll be saving them, Ivor."

"The risk is too great."

"Will you at least listen to me?"

Chief Superintendent Griffith paused a long time before he said, "Okay. Talk to me."

20
A Study in Scarlet

Morgan paused in the lobby of New Scotland Yard to light a pipe and appreciate the eternal flame dedicated to the memory of Scotland Yarders who died in the line of duty. The glass-encased memorial was the only distinguishing feature of the lobby. The young constable who had driven him to the Yard now waited restlessly beside the unmarked police car outside. When Morgan came out he stood up straight and Morgan expected him to salute. "I thank you for waiting, Constable, but I believe I'll walk back to the hotel."

"That's a bit of a stroll, sir."

"Got some thinking to do." Morgan smiled. As he turned from Broadway onto Victoria Street, Big Ben rang five times. A few minutes later he crossed the square in front of Westminster Abbey and only a moment later Broad Sanctuary where at one corner of a small park stood a glowering statue of Sir Winston Churchill, his eyes fixed on the tower of Big Ben and the Houses of Parliament. He paused a moment to admire the clock tower, then used the subway to avoid the blur of going-home traffic streaming around Westminster Bridge. On Whitehall, he walked north, pausing only a moment at the corner of Derby Gate to look down the slight incline to the gates behind which stood the Scotland Yard vacated in favor of the nondescript

building he had just left. Walking again, he was mindful
of the other buildings of Her Majesty's Government, of
the opening into Downing Street and of the formidable
structure housing the Foreign Office, which in
Holmes's day, according to Dr. Watson, relied so heavily upon the brilliance of Holmes's brother, Mycroft.

Across Whitehall, Morgan cut through the courtyards
of the Queen's Horse Guards and chuckled at a knot of
tourists posing for photographs beside the sleek black
horses with their red-white-black-and-silver uniformed
riders. Behind the Horse Guards he crossed toward St.
James's Park, walking faster now, and arrived at the
imposing flight of steps beneath the column holding at
its top a statue of the Duke of York. Behind it, he
strolled across Waterloo Place to Pall Mall, turned west
and thought again of Mycroft Holmes, whose club, Di-
ogenes, had been located there.

**It was as he turned to pass St. James's Square
that the lean and hawkish man who had been accom-
panying him spoke: "It's a good plan, Morgan. Carries
a bit of a risk, but I would say it's worth the candle."**

**"I'm playing fast and loose with lives in this, my
friend."**

"So is your adversary."

**"A hellish way to murder someone," Morgan mut-
tered. "Ethan Remarque was a fine man. I'm dealing
with a madman, of course."**

**"Murder is not the act of a sane mind, ever, I'm
afraid."**

**Morgan crossed Piccadilly in front of the Ritz
Hotel with its white bulbs glowing warmly in the chill-
ing dusk. The windows of shops and travel offices**

along Berkeley Street looked bright, cozy, and inviting. Presently, opposite the May Fair Hotel, Morgan paused. "Leslie Westin is staying there."

"Certainly you've discounted him as a factor by now."

Berkeley Square beneath its wintry trees was empty, its benches deserted, its paths aswirl with dried leaves and dust kicked up by a rising wind. "General de Merville lived here in *The Adventure of the Illustrious Client,* if I remember my Canon."

"And Admiral Sinclair had a house on this square. He figured in the Bruce-Partington plans case."

At Grosvenor Square, Morgan looked at his companion, who had been silent for some minutes. His gray eyes were turned toward the west side of the square at a long modern building topped by an enormous spread-winged eagle. "The residence of the American ambassador. It's always been a deep regret on my part that the foolish policies of a British King brought about the separation of our two peoples."

Morgan cut through Grosvenor Square Park to look at the monument to Franklin Delano Roosevelt. "Did you know he was an Irregular?"

"If I did not know I would surely deduce it to be so."

"F.D.R. had the idea that you were an American. In a little piece he wrote for the *Baker Street Journal* he insisted that your attributes were primarily American, not English."

"I found that both amusing and immensely flattering."

"Are you amazed that you are alive—and real—for so many people?"

"I try not to be amazed, Morgan."
"Will you come to Baskerville Hall?"
"It remains to be seen."

At Durrants Hotel, Morgan found the Men of Tor engrossed in a game of poker in front of a roaring fireplace in the writing room. Carrie Lonsback sat nearby kibbitzing. Wiggins glanced up from a possible straight. "No need to count heads, Morgan. We're all here, all alive. What did the chief superintendent want?"

"He wanted to show me the official report on Ethan's death."

"And what was the verdict?"

"A massive stroke."

"And you believed it?"

Morgan's eyes roamed the faces of the Men of Tor. "What choice do I have?"

"Do you recommend that we swallow this balderdash?"

"That's your affair, Wiggy. I've learned never to tell you anything."

"Are you going to drop your investigation? Will you pack and go home? Decamp?"

"Hell, no. I'm going to dinner tonight at the Sherlock Holmes Pub and tomorrow I'm going to Baskerville Hall."

"Ah, the chief superintendent has given us leave to depart London?"

"I suspect the chief superintendent will be delighted to get us out of his hair."

"The man," growled Wiggins, slowly shaking his huge head, "is a bigger fool than Lestrade ever was."

Morgan looked at his watch. "We'll have to hurry or we'll forfeit our reservations at the pub."

"Except for Baker Street, no other section of London is so identified with Holmes as the area around Charing Cross Station," lectured B. Alexander Wiggins for the benefit of Carrie Lonsback as she and Morgan shared a taxi to the Sherlock Holmes Pub. "Number ten, which is the address of the pub and restaurant, was once the location of the Northumberland Arms Hotel. It was there that Holmes picked up the first clue that allowed him to unravel the mystery of *The Hound of The Baskervilles.* Nearby was the Charing Cross Hotel, where Oberstein was captured in the smoking room in *The Bruce-Partington Plans.* And, of course, Stapleton stayed at the Mexborough Hotel in the same *Hound of the Baskervilles.* Holmes and Watson were quite familiar with the area and often used Charing Cross Station. In fact, Mathews knocked out Holmes's left canine tooth there in *The Empty House.* Also on Northumberland Avenue we find the Turkish bath establishment of *The Illustrious Client.* And within a stone's throw is Whitehall and the offices of Her Majesty's Government, which, as we all know, often rested wholly in the capable hands of Sherlock's brother, Mycroft. There is much in the neighborhood to consider including in planning the instructive tours which have brought us to London in spite of the deadly peril we are all in."

The taxi drew up in front of the pub, a four-story brickface building, the lower part of which was of green-painted wood with gold trim. The bottom panes of glass in two large windows were frosted and depicted scenes of several Holmesian adventures. In yellow-and-red letters above the windows and doors, the name of the pub was inscribed. Over the sidewalk hung a Whitbread pub sign with the aquiline profile of Holmes painted upon it. A few moments later, a second cab carrying the remaining Men of Tor drew up to the curb.

Immediately, they entered the pub and went upstairs to the restaurant above. "Tight squeeze for you, Wiggins," said Ben Artnikoff, leading the way up to a landing and up again to the door to the restaurant. "Good evening," said Artnikoff to the woman who greeted him as he went in, "we are the party which has reserved the tables beside the study."

"It's all prepared, sir," she smiled. "Each of you will have an unobstructed view inside." She held out her left arm, indicating the way to the tables.

As they arranged themselves, Wiggins lectured again. "The study was commissioned by the Conan Doyle estate. It was commissioned in 1951 for the Festival of Britain and has been installed here for posterity, and for us." He flung both hands toward the plate glass separating the dining room from the re-created room. "221–B Baker Street!"

Carrie Lonsback stifled a giggle as a solemn hush fell upon the five Men of Tor and Morgan, but as she peered into the room beyond the glass her own face settled into its own solemnity. Morgan noticed and was touched by it. Before them lay an extraordinary scene. The immediate impression was of the color red. A study in scarlet, Morgan thought—a private, silent joke. It was a Victorian room cluttered with the items which any Sherlockian would recognize, but presently Morgan decided he ought to instruct Carrie Lonsback on the subtleties of the marvelous room. Softly, as if he were speaking in church, he pointed out the table in the corner with a forest of bottles, jars, beakers, and laboratory glasses which constituted Holmes's personal science lab. Above it hung shelves festooned with bottles bearing labels specifying the Sherlockian experiments which they contained. Next to the chemistry corner stood a wax effigy of Holmes complete with checkered dressing gown and a bullet hole in the forehead. "That was Moran's bullet, you'll recall," he whispered. Behind the figure of Holmes was a window which, if one could look through it, promised a view of Baker Street in 1895. In a wall to the left was a fireplace and upon it were more of Holmes's possessions—a clock, the Persian slipper which he kept his tobacco in, a bellows, a rack of pipes, and a heap of papers on which Holmes had probably jotted important things to be remembered. Before the hearth, arranged for the great sleuth's ease and convenience were chairs and tables, each of them burdened by items which Holmes might have just laid down or cast aside. "Not a very neat housekeeper," Morgan said. "He drove Mrs. Hudson and Watson frantic, but of course, neither would dare touch anything." On the opposite wall next to the door to 221–B were holes in the shape of the letters *V* and *R*. "Target practice with a little bow to Victoria Regina," explained Morgan. Immediately on the opposite side of the glass separating them from the study stood a littered table. Conspicuous among the items on it was a small case containing the implements which

Holmes needed for the taking of cocaine. "A seven-percent solution," Morgan said. "Watson was quite put off by it and delivered stern rebukes to Holmes. With little effect."

Carrie Lonsback sighed. "I wish . . ."

Amused, Morgan asked, "You wish what?"

With effort, she said, "I wish Ethan were here."

"Ah, yes." Morgan nodded.

A waitress broke the unexpected gloom by passing around menus. From the wide array of choices there could be only one dish for all of them. "The Chicken Sherlock Holmes," announced Wiggins immediately. The others quickly made it unanimous. Ben Artnikoff ordered the wine. Throwing medical prudence to the wind, Cliff Brownglass insisted on wine, as well. "I will not sit in front of Holmes's study and sip diet ginger ale!"

Chicken Sherlock Holmes was demi-glacé in a mush-room, onion, and red wine sauce. Peas and rice accom-panied it. Ben Artnikoff's wine was Premières Côtes de Bordeaux. Desserts from a trolley were Apricot Bou-chees, various tarts, Orange cake, and St. Honoré Trifle. Coffee was American.

With cognac bought by Morgan in a burst of extrava-gance they toasted Herman Sloan and Ethan Cage Re-marque.

Then lifting his glass again, Wiggins proposed, "To Holmes."

Benjamin Artnikoff followed with a toast to Watson. "The great sleuth's Boswell!"

"That long-suffering woman—Mrs. Hudson," said James Donald Cape.

"And to the truly smart one in the family," said Bill Miner. "Mycroft Holmes."

Remembering his realm of Sherlockian expertise, Cliff Brownglass said, "To Basil Rathbone and Nigel Bruce."

Wiggins turned to Carrie Lonsback. "Have you someone to toast, my dear?"

Hesitantly, glancing around the table, she asked, "Might I suggest a toast to the real Sherlock Holmes?"

"Hear, hear," Wiggins said. "To Dr. Joseph Bell."

"No, no. I meant Sir Arthur Conan Doyle."

"Of course!" Benjamin Artnikoff laughed. "To *him*, too."

21
The Resident Patient

At four o'clock in the morning Morgan was jolted awake by Kenny West via trans-Atlantic telephone. "I didn't think you'd be at your hotel, Dave. Figured I'd have to leave a message."

"Why'n hell wouldn't I be here? Do you know what time it is?"

"Well, it's eleven o'clock here in Boston. Since you're five hours behind U.S. time . . ."

Morgan groaned. "Britain is *ahead*, Kenny."

"Oh, so I woke you up . . ."

"At four in the morning."

Kenny moaned. "Sorry, Dave."

"Now that I'm awake, what have you got for me?"

"Bad news. Joseph Bell is not your man. He happens to be an inmate at a mental hospital in Cambridge."

"Are you certain it's our Joseph Bell?"

"No doubt about it, Dave. I've been following the trail of the Bell family all over Massachusetts. They lived in Lowell for a time, then in Gloucester, and finally Cambridge. During all that time Bell was getting progressively batty. Finally he just flipped out altogether and the family put him in storage."

"And Bell is still tucked away?"

"There's no way he could have been on Long Island shooting at Herman Sloan or in Manhattan pelting your friend Wiggins with sticks."

"He could have had others do it."

"Dave, the man is totally wigged-out. Talks gibberish. Throws fits. Most of the time they have him tied to a bed and loaded with dope. From what I've been able to determine he's been in and out of loony bins for years. Delusions. A real schizo, apparently. Finally, his family had to institutionalize him."

"Have you talked to the family?"

"Their last known address was Cambridge. That's where Bell was taken away by the men in white coats. No forwarding address. The staff at the hospital says Mrs. Bell used to visit regularly but she hasn't been in for months. Theory is she's dead. I have no idea where the Bell family is. Some neighbors I talked to said one son named Kevin was a dropout back in the sixties and just vanished. A second son, Lex, went the other route

and joined the Marines. Duty around the world. No
one's seen him for ages. A third son named Carl or
Calvin, the Cambridge neighbors never saw. The Bell
family was not what you'd consider friendly. The folks
I talked to had the impression that Mrs. Bell was
ashamed because her husband was nuts. The way I
figure it, Bell really did think he was a great Sherlockian
scholar and wasn't trying to con anybody when your
pals gave him the boot from the Irregulars. Anyway, it
looks like the Bell angle is a dead end."

"Sorry for the wild-goose chase, Kenny."

"Well, that's what I get paid for, hunh? It's too
bad. Bell was my favorite suspect. What's new on your
end?"

"Ethan Remarque is dead."

"Holy Christ. Was he . . .?

"Yes. Poison administered with a hypodermic. As
close as the killer could come to making it look like the
snake-bite death in *The Speckled Band.*"

"How'd your traveling companions take that bit of
news?"

"They've been told by Scotland Yard that Ethan died
of natural causes. My old friend Ivor Griffith is cooper-
ating with me."

"Ah, you've got a plan, eh?"

"Some plan! It amounts to pushing ahead with our
visit to Baskerville Hall in the *hope* that whoever's
doing this will slip up. It's a risk."

"What else can you do, hunh?"

"I'm going to find this killer, Kenny. Ethan's death
was my fault. I knew he wanted to talk to me. I let it
slide. I didn't believe there was someone out to kill the
Men of Tor. I figured that we were all the victims of

a badly-timed set of coincidences and a practical joke. Now I know better. Had I been sharper, more alert . . ."

"Dave, you can't blame yourself."

"But I do, Kenny. I do."

"Is there anything more I can do on my end?"

"It doesn't look that way. Take a couple of days off. Enjoy New England. Get in some skiing."

"Okay if I call you in a day or two? Just to keep in touch?"

"Sure. I'll be at Baskerville Hall."

"I'll try to remember that you're ahead of me in time," Kenny said, repentantly.

Morgan put down the phone with an amusing but macabre thought. In the morning he would be heading back in time, back to the dark and mysterious days when Sherlock Holmes prowled the dismal and fetid moor surrounding the ancestral home of the Baskervilles whose fate it was to be dogged through all their generations by a fiendish curse. That bleak and bloody legend was kept alive by Sir Malcolm Bannister in a country estate which was nothing less than a faithful re-creation of Baskerville Hall and which would now be the stage upon which *The Adventure of Murder Most Irregular* would be played through to the final curtain. "Yes," he said aloud as he turned out the light, "I believe we are about to begin the final act."

He slept quite peacefully until the wake-up buzzer went off at seven o'clock. Dressing, he wished he had a Watson to whom he could turn and cry, "Come, old fellow. We have, I think, just time to catch our train."

22
Train From Paddington

In the abundantly romantic lore of railroads there have been many fabulous terminals. In New York City, Penn Station from which rolled the great trains of the Pennsylvania Railroad and Grand Central Terminal out of which roared the Twentieth Century Limited. In Paris, the Gare de l'Est from whose main platform departed a long, luxurious train belonging to the Compagnie Internationale des Wagons-Lits et des Grands Express Européens—also known as the Orient Express. But no city boasts as many romantic railway stations as London: Victoria, Charing Cross, Euston, Waterloo, King's Cross, Marylebone, St. Pancras, Liverpool, Broad Street, and Paddington. When it was the London terminus of the Great Western Railway, Paddington Station lay close to Baker Street and it was from there that Sherlock Holmes boarded trains for the Boscombe Valley and Exeter in the investigation of cases and it was Paddington Station which afforded rail service to Devonshire and the estate of Sir Henry Baskerville.

"There is no coincidence in the fact that many Sherlockians are also railwayists," said Morgan as he helped Carrie Lonsback from a taxi at Paddington Station. "Holmes was a chronic user of the railroads in his time and quite an expert on them. It's known that he timed a train while on his way to investigate the mystery of

Silver Blaze. He pointed out to Watson that the tele-
graph posts upon the line were sixty yards apart and
that calculating a train's speed was easy for that reason.
In *The Norwood Builders* Holmes deduced that writing
on several scraps of paper had been done on a train.
The writing was good in stations, bad when the train
was moving, and very bad when it crossed over
switches, or points, as the British call them." Morgan
gazed up at the façade of Paddington Station. "It's kind
of a thrill to be arriving at this depot on our way to
Baskerville Hall, just as Holmes did so long ago." He
glanced at Carrie Lonsback and grinned. "One almost
wishes that there'd be a gigantic hound of Hell waiting
for us when we arrive."

The Men of Tor piled from taxis and milled around
their luggage as porters loaded the valises onto carts.
Presently, with British efficiency and courtesy, the luggage was stowed in two adjoining first class compart-
ments reserved for the Men of Tor, Carrie Lonsback,
and Morgan. Because of his size, Wiggins shared with
Carrie Lonsback and Morgan, occupying one of the
seats himself and riding backward as the train eased out
of Paddington Station. "I feel decidedly more comfortable than Watson," announced Wiggins as the train
came out from under the roof of the terminal and into
the dull sunlight of the wintry morning.

"Why is that?" asked Carrie Lonsback.

"Well, Watson when he went to Baskerville Hall
went alone. Holmes remained in London. Or so it
seemed. I have my modern-day Sherlock Holmes with
me on the journey."

"Flattery will get you anything, Wiggy," admonished
Morgan.

"You said it *seemed* that Holmes stayed behind in London?" asked Carrie Lonsback.

"Holmes went to Baskerville Hall, of course," explained Morgan, "but he wanted it to appear that he was staying in London for a few days. That permitted him to investigate the mystery in secret."

"His presence on the moor came as quite a surprise to Watson when the good doctor went out in search of a mysterious man who had been seen on Tor. Tor is the predominate geological feature of the moor, a great outcropping of rock. Holmes holed up in a cave there while carrying out his investigations. So you can understand, Miss Lonsback, why the B.S.I.'s Investiture of Man of Tor is especially valued. It stands for Holmes, himself."

Wiggins bent forward as much as his girth permitted and patted Morgan on the knee. "David's Investiture is Wilson Hargreave, the New York police detective."

Carrie Lonsback turned to Morgan with a smile. "I'm sure if Mr. Holmes were alive day he wouldn't hesitate to cable David Morgan for assistance."

"*If* Holmes were alive today? But he is!" Wiggins exclaimed as he reared back laughing.

As the train rolled slowly out of Paddington Station, Benjamin Artnikoff poked his whiskered face into the compartment and wiggled a finger at Morgan. "May I see you a moment, David?" When Morgan stepped into the passageway, Artnikoff closed the sliding door. Taking Morgan's arm, he said, "If we could step between the cars?"

"What's up, Ben?"

Artnikoff waited until they stood between the swaying railroad carriages before he reached into his pocket and withdrew an envelope. "This was slipped under my door during the night."

Morgan opened the envelope and withdrew a slip of paper. On it he found a string of stick-figures. "Christ."

"*The Adventure of the Dancing Men.* You recall the method of death in the story?"

"Mr. Hilton Cubitt was shot to death."

"I presume that this little example of Holmesian artwork is a forecast of my own death by gunshot."

"Or another joke."

"Really, Morgan."

"Have you told the others about this?"

"Certainly not."

"Don't. Okay?"

Ben Artnikoff smiled. "That was a pretty song and dance you performed at breakfast yesterday. Not for a second did I believe you. The men of Scotland Yard may believe that Ethan died naturally. You don't."

"No, I don't, Ben."

"I shan't ask you what you're up to."

"Thank you."

"It's quite sad, realizing that one of the Men of Tor is a murderer, but how can we escape that conclusion, eh?"

"I'm keeping an open mind on that."

"Are you still seriously considering Westin and Hess-Feldstein as suspects? Preposterous. Our murderer is among us, Morgan. This—" he took the dancing men from Morgan—"is the proof of it."

"You could have drawn the dancing men yourself, Ben."

Tucking the paper back into his pocket, Artnikoff

smiled. "Suspect all of us, Morgan. Trust no one."

"Thanks for the advice, Ben. I appreciate it."

"You're very cool, Morgan. To look at you no one would detect the slightest hint of how your mind is working. You're very good. My compliments. Incidentally, I think Miss Lonsback ought to turn back. She has no place in this."

"I believe that's entirely up to her, Ben."

"True," he smiled. "Just a thought."

Wiggins was dozing when Morgan returned to his compartment but Carrie Lonsback was awake, her face a study in worry. "What is it, David? What did Mr. Artnikoff want?"

Morgan sat and peered out the window at London neighborhoods flashing past the train. "He's worried about you."

"About me?"

"He suggested that it might be wise if you returned home."

"Did he? The nerve."

"He was just being considerate."

"Well, tell him I'm a big girl and can take care of myself."

Morgan smiled. "That is the one obvious fact in this entire adventure, Miss Lonsback."

"If you truly believe that, why have you been lying to me?"

"Lying? When?"

"It's a lie when you say that you believe Mr. Remarque died of natural causes. You know he was murdered. Wiggins was not the victim of a mugging. He was deliberately attacked by the same person who killed Mr. Remarque and Mr. Sloan in New York. Honestly, David, no one believes you when you pretend otherwise. I'm appalled that Scotland Yard has been deceived."

"They're professional policemen trained to deal with facts. As far as they're concerned, Ethan passed away in his sleep."

"Then you're left on your own to find the murderer. Is that it?"

"In a nutshell."

"I want to help you, David. If I can."

"Then take Ben Artnikoff's advice. This is no place for a . . ."

"For a woman? God, I ought to slap your face for that."

"I apologize."

"I'm an able person, David. If I can be of help to you, I want to be. Even your hero, Sherlock Holmes, had help from Dr. Watson. Whether you let me help you or not, I am going to Baskerville Hall and nothing can persuade me otherwise."

"I won't even try."

Presently, the train left behind the rooftops and chimneys of the city of London and its picturesque suburbs and was winding across a wintry landscape of gently rolling hills, stark leafless woods, and fields of frozen brown soil divided by hedgerows where snow lay underneath like lace trim. Gently rocked by the swaying of the train, Wiggins and Carrie Lonsback slept. When Morgan left for the amenity known in Britain as a water-closet, he glanced into the adjoining compartment and found all the Men of Tor except Bill Miner asleep. Immediately Miner stepped from the compartment and gently closed the sliding door. "I have to talk to you," he whispered. Taking Morgan's arm, he said, "Not here."

In the vestibule at the front of the carriage, Morgan asked, "What is it, Bill?"

Miner rubbed a hand nervously against his chin. "Someone tried to get into my room last night."

"Are you certain?"

"Yes. Tried the latch a couple of times. I could see a shadow beneath the door. I turned on the light in my room and a few seconds later heard a door open and close down the hall. There's only one of the others with a room on my floor. I'm certain that's who was trying to get into my room to . . ."

"Calm down, Bill."

"Until last night, when he tried to get into my room, I thought we were all victims of a practical joker whose pranks happened to coincide with the two deaths and the attack on Wiggins. But now I'm convinced Herm was murdered. So was Ethan, no matter what Scotland Yard thinks. And the killer is not one of those outsiders. Not Bell, not Hess-Feldstein, nor Westin. He's one of us. God, it's a terrible thing to have to say. To accuse . . ."

"Accuse whom, Bill?"

"Jimmy Cape."

"On what evidence?"

Miner turned away with a groan. "It sounds so damned ridiculous."

"Nothing's ridiculous if it leads to murder."

Miner turned back. "Do you agree that Herm and Ethan were murdered?"

"I didn't say that. What I care about is that you believe it and that you believe you know who might have done it. Why Jimmy Cape?"

"It's me he's after. He's doing what Ben Artnikoff often jokes about. If you want to kill someone, kill many so the body will get lost in a crowd. That's what Jimmy's doing."

"*Why,* Bill?"

"If I'm dead he'll be able to get his hands on something he's wanted for years. My complete collection of *The Strand.*"

"Come on, Bill. Cape's got enough money to buy *The Strand* from half a dozen collectors or to scrounge the world for single copies until he's got them all."

"Ah, but many of the copies in my collection are signed by Conan Doyle himself."

"No one kills for Conan Doyle's signature."

"I said it sounds damned ridiculous but if I die Cape will get the collection."

"Is he in your will?"

"No, but my son is. You know my son. Flighty. No sense of responsibility. Wants to live high on the hog. Cape would make my son an offer even before they lowered me into my grave and my son would snap it up like that."

"But to kill others just to conceal your death? For a handful of magazines?"

"*The Strand,* Morgan! Signed by Conan Doyle. Ah, you take it lightly. This little cult of Sherlock Holmes is a diversion for you. Like your model trains. But for others—many others—it's an obsession. It's been an obsession for Jimmy Cape for years. Now, I'm afraid, that obsession has gone over the line into madness."

"Then why don't you go back home? Why continue on this trip?"

Miner laughed bitterly. "He'd only kill me there. He means to kill me, Morgan. He'll try at Sir Malcolm's. The fact that you came on this trip tells me that you take all of this seriously. In all candor, I feel safer continuing on the trip because you're with us than I would feel if I went back home. Jimmy Cape is the man, Morgan. I'm certain of it. Watch him. I know I will. Now, I'd better get back to my compartment. Please wait a few minutes before you return. I don't want him to know I've been talking to you."

Hurrying, struggling to keep his footing as the speeding train swayed and lurched on its run through the countryside of Devon, Bill Miner was as frightened a man as Morgan had ever seen, and as Miner ducked into the compartment where Ben Artnikoff, Cliff Browning, and James Donald Cape slept, Morgan felt a rush of hatred that was new and frightening to him, a hatred of the person who had committed two murders and attempted a third but who had committed another crime in the process, one almost as heinous as the crime of homicide. The anonymous plotter of a scheme worthy of Professor Moriarty had turned the Men of Tor against each other, made them fear each other and made a mockery of a genial comradeship that had previously bound them together as brothers.

Wiggins still slept but Carrie Lonsback was awake and peering through the window at Devonshire. She glanced at Morgan, smiled, then looked out the window again. "It's very beautiful, isn't it?" Morgan slumped onto the seat. Turning to him, she asked, "What's wrong, David?"

" 'There's the scarlet thread of murder running through the colorless skein of life,' " he replied.

" 'And our duty is to unravel it, and isolate it, and expose every inch of it.' " Wiggins was awake. The great pumpkinlike head turned slowly toward the view through the window. "We are nearly there, Morgan."

"Nearly there but not yet," muttered Morgan.

Wiggins heaved himself closer to the window, his round face almost pressed against the pane. "We are coming to the edge of the moor."

Looking out, Morgan stared across the chilled Devon fields and beyond a low curve of woods to a gray and melancholy hill with a strange jagged summit, dim and vague in the distance like a lunar landscape. "Tor?" asked Morgan.

"Yes," nodded Wiggins.

Morgan gazed and in his mind he was once more a boy searching rows upon rows of dusty books and reaching for a slender volume which he hoped would prove to be an escape from the labors of studies but which, amazingly, had been the beginning of the skein of his own life and which had brought him to the very place where, so long ago, the ground had been impressed with the footprints of a gigantic hound.

III

Baskerville Hall

23
Twice-Told Tale

"How quaint," Carrie Lonsback said.

"God." Ben Artnikoff laughed. "I never expected
this."

"Typical of Sir Malcolm," said Wiggins.

"Marvelous," said James Donald Cape.

Bill Miner shook his head.

Cliff Brownglass gave a delighted clap of hands. "Terrific."

"The right touch," Morgan said approvingly.

Before them as they stepped from the train at a small
way-station bearing the name BASKERVILLE HALL they
found a pair of four-wheelers, their leather tops folded
back, their black enamel sides gleaming, their gilt-
trimmed doors opened, their white horses pawing the
hard earth and breathing gusts of steam, and two young
drivers liveried in Victorian elegance beside each carriage. One of them, a tall blond youth in red coat, gray
pants, gleaming black boots, and wearing a crisp brown
beaver tophat, stepped forward. "Sir Malcolm wel-
comes you to Baskerville Hall."

Behind the carriages a small Chevrolet station wagon
waited to receive their luggage. Boarding the first of
the carriages, Wiggins seated himself regally and gazed

disapprovingly at the automobile. "Curse the twentieth century!"

The blond youth held out a hand to assist Carrie Lonsback into the carriage. Beside Wiggins, she seemed as tiny as a doll. Morgan followed her into the carriage. The young driver mounted the box. "If you get cold crossing the moor there are blankets. Or I could put up the top."

"This is fine," Carrie Lonsback said.

"Fine? It's perfect," exclaimed Wiggins.

"Okay, folks, here we go," said the driver, snapping the reins.

"To Baskerville Hall," Wiggins cried excitedly.

The carriages rattled onto a macadam road. As the station wagon with their luggage sped away, the roar of its engine faded quickly leaving only the sound of the horses' hooves, the metallic rolling of the carriage wheels and the whisper of the wind in trees lining the winding country road. A pale sun struggled vainly to break through gray clouds. Little piles of snow lay protected by the skirts of hedges.

"It's as if we'd been swept back in time," said Carrie Lonsback.

"Back to the days of the great Holmes himself," said Wiggins with a nod. "One can see Watson and the others in a carriage like this and hear the excitement in Sir Henry Baskerville's voice as he neared his ancestral home for the first time. Imagine his excitement. Plus the added thrill of knowing he was in danger of his life. Do you know the story, Miss Lonsback?"

"Vaguely. Something to do with a mad dog."

"A dog? A hound, Miss Lonsback. To say that *The*

Hound of the Baskervilles concerns a dog is to say that *War and Peace* is about Russia."

"You're dying to tell the story, Wiggins, so get on with it." Morgan laughed.

"In the time of the Great Rebellion, Hugo Baskerville, a cruel and profane man, kidnapped the beautiful daughter of a yeoman and held her prisoner. But the young woman escaped. Hugo Baskerville was furious. Pursuing her, he cried out that he would give his soul if he might overtake and kill the wench. When Hugo's friends caught up with the man they were horrified to see him being attacked by a giant hound. The animal ripped Hugo Baskerville's throat to shreds. The spectral hound was a perennial curse of succeeding Baskervilles. In the case which Holmes investigated, it was Sir Charles Baskerville who died of a heart attack while running to escape the hound. I shan't tell you the ending. You must read Watson for that."

"Arthur Conan Doyle had quite an imagination," said Carrie Lonsback.

"Well, it wasn't all imagination, you see. Hugo Baskerville was based on Richard Cabell, a seventeenth-century heir to the manor of Brook. Like Sir Hugo, Cabell was a profane and brutal man. He suspected his wife of sleeping with a man from the nearby town of Buckfastleigh. Cabell beat the woman unmercifully. She ran off across the moor. He followed in a fury. When he caught her, he stabbed her to death. The woman's hound flew at Cabell and tore out his throat. Legend had it that the hound prowled the moor for centuries thereafter, howling horribly, and attacking Cabell's descendants. Conan Doyle heard of this story, remembered it, and turned it into the masterpiece we all know and love. Conan Doyle was fond of dogs. He used them in several stories, ranging from the faithful bloodhound called Toby which Holmes borrowed from time to time to track criminals, the great hound of Hell tormenting the Baskervilles, to the dog in *Silver Blaze.* "

"Silent watchdogs and howling hounds. Quite a menagerie," she said.

"Sir Malcolm Bannister is an animal fancier, as well. Horses. There are the really fine pairs pulling these wonderful coaches. And he has a small stable of thoroughbred racers. Not unexpectedly one of them is named Silver Blaze," said Wiggins. "I suppose Jimmy Cape will insist on riding Silver Blaze."

"Sir Malcolm has no hounds?" Morgan asked.

"Oh, he has dozens. This is hunt country, and Sir Malcolm is a man who observes the traditions. No reason to fear the dogs, however. They're quite friendly. Unless you happen to be a fox." Wiggins laughed and rolled his great head to take in the vast, rolling sprawl of the moor.

Carrie Lonsback shuddered. "Got a chill?" Morgan asked.

"A little."

Morgan unfolded a gray tartan lap blanket and tucked it around her. When she touched his hand and held it, he made no effort to withdraw it. Noticing, Wiggins smiled slightly. Morgan blushed.

Wiggins turned again to study the moor. "I expect that it was much like this as Watson, Dr. Mortimer, and Sir Henry Baskerville made their way to Baskerville Hall while Holmes pretended to remain behind in London. A desolate place but strangely beautiful and allur-

ing." He glanced at Carrie Lonsback with upraised eye-
brows. "But beware of the great Grimpen Mire. A
treacherous morass that can suck a man into it like
quicksand, eh, Morgan? With the possible exception of
Count Dracula's castle, I can think of no place more
suited for a tale of murder and ancestral curses."

Carrie Lonsback shuddered again and tightened her
hand on Morgan's.

As the carriages drew up before the steps of the old
country mansion renamed Baskerville Hall, Sir Malcolm Bannister stepped through the door and down the
steps. Tall, silver-haired, as lean and hawk-nosed as
Sherlock Holmes himself, Sir Malcolm was dressed for
the country in tan jodhpurs, a green tartan shirt with
a green silk ascot, and a dark brown coat with leather
patches at the elbows. He puffed on a golden-brown
Calabash pipe. "Ah, you are here! What a pretty picture
you all are! A study for Sidney Paget's pencil and pad
if ever there were one. Welcome to Baskerville Hall."
Carrie Lonsback did the introductions. "A late addition
to the guest list, Mr. Morgan," he said as they shook
hands, "but we could house a small regiment, I suspect.
Please consider my household staff at your disposal. My
late wife used to chastise me for having so many staff,
but, my friends, I would be lost without help. I don't
cook, find the making up of a bed a mystery, know
nothing whatsoever about fixing things, and until quite
recently did not know how to drive an auto. In short,
I have nothing to recommend me except a title, a small
fortune wrenched from the ground in South Africa by
my ancestors, and an abiding interest in the cause of
Sherlock Holmes. It is this which is my only truly re-

deeming characteristic. I'm regarded by my neighbors as an eccentric old physician but they grudgingly admit that my eccentricity has turned a rundown old barn of a house into a showpiece. I hope you'll find Baskerville Hall hospitable and exciting and I hope that within its walls we shall work out the details of our little business enterprise to everyone's satisfaction."

Sir Malcolm clapped his hands and a moment later a young man in the Victorian clothing of a butler appeared. "Sir?"

"My guests are ready to go to their rooms to freshen up and rest." Sir Malcolm smiled at each of the guests. "Dinner will be at eight. This young man—Alexander is his name—will come to collect you in time. If you wish or need anything, just give the cord in your rooms a little tug and Alexander will respond. For our first meal together I've arranged a repast that would do honor to Sir Hugo himself."

24
Lord of the Manor

Shortly before eight, Morgan sought Sir Malcolm Bannister in the library of Baskerville Hall. A new fire blazed behind the high iron dogs of the hearth as Sir Malcolm poked at the huge logs. He did not look up as Morgan came into the room. "I hope everything is satisfactory."

"It's fine, Sir Malcolm."

Straightening, Sir Malcolm placed the poker into a rack of fireplace implements and reached into the pocket of his gray tweed jacket to withdraw an amber pipe. "A dreadful thing, the death of Ethan Remarque. We were correspondents and I owe a good deal of the inspiration for Baskerville Hall to him. I never met Mr. Sloan, but I gather he was a first rate Sherlockian."

"One of the best."

Sir Malcolm struck a match to his pipe. Puffing, he said, "I hope we come to a satisfactory conclusion of the business which brought you here under these melancholy conditions."

"I'm sure we will, Sir Malcolm."

"You're sure everything's satisfactory?"

"I am, indeed."

"I don't mind telling you I feel rather awkward."

"That is certainly understandable."

Sir Malcolm indicated a chair for Morgan and they sat near the fire facing each other. Morgan packed and lit a bent black briar pipe. "Ah, you're a pipe smoker. I ought to have known. I believe that the majority of Sherlockians indulge. 'A pipe! It is a great soother, a pleasant comforter! Blue devils fly before its honest breath! It ripens the brain—it opens the heart; and the man who smokes, thinks like a sage and acts like a Samaritan!' "

"If that's from The Canon, I don't recall it."

"Oh, no. Edward Bulwer, *Night and Morning*, 1851. A few years before Holmes's time." Sir Malcolm drew

a satisfying mouthful of smoke from his amber and ex-
haled slowly. "I wonder why Holmes never wrote a
monograph on pipes as he did on tobacco?"

"Perhaps he did but Watson overlooked mentioning
it."

"There was very little that Watson overlooked of importance, I think. As you are a detective, I suspect there
is little of importance that you overlook."

"I appreciate the confidence but my kind of detective work is a far cry from Holmes's. My cases are rather
routine affairs. Divorces. Industrial espionage. Anti-
terrorist protection."

"It sounds perfectly thrilling to me. I'm stuck out
here in the moor with my books and my manuscripts."

"Ah, but what a project you've undertaken. Restora-
tion of this old manor house. You've done a magnificent
job."

Proudly, Sir Malcolm looked around the library. "It's
getting into shape. Thank God the builders and paint-
ers are gone. Now it's only the household staff who
track in mud and bump into the furniture. The great
pity of our twentieth-century headlong rush into de-
mocracy, Mr. Morgan, is the disappearance of a servant
class. Being an American and so young you have little
knowledge, I'm sure, of the way it used to be. Being a
servant was not considered work beneath someone's
dignity. The job passed from one generation to another.
Believe me when I tell you that the British Empire
rested as much upon the pride and devotion of the
servant class as it rested upon the aristocracy who
trained for empire on the playing fields of Eton."

"Your staff seems quite capable."

"Ah, but the training that is required! For them it

seems to be a lark, even with the rather handsome
wages I pay. I'm not sure if they will wish to make a
career of it. I suspect I am doomed to constantly training new help. What I would give for the kind of serv-
ants I knew when I was a child. But those days are gone.
Alas, the Age of Victoria has disappeared."

"One of your coachmen is an American?"

"Ah, you are sharp. Yes. His name is Robert. He is
marvelous with animals. Takes charge of the horses and
seems to enjoy the work."

"How long has he been working for you?"

"Why, I don't exactly recall. Over a year, I suppose.
Why do you ask?"

"Plain old-fashioned curiosity. Detectives are like
cats when it comes to curiosity.

"Well, I hope you are like the cat in relation to having
numerous lives, Mr. Morgan."

"Your idea of having us met at the train station by
four-wheelers was an inspiration."

"An experiment, really. I wondered if it might be-
come a part of the routine when persons come to visit
Baskerville Hall. It would serve to put guests into a
Victorian frame of mind, don't you agree?"

"It's pure genius, Sir Malcolm. And Durrants Hotel is
the right place for them to stay in London. It's been
your favorite for some time, I was told."

"A wonderful hotel. Did you know that it served as
a model for Agatha Christie in her Jane Marpel novel,
At Bertram's Hotel?"

"I didn't. I'll have to read it and see if I recognize the
place."

"Oh you will. I knew Dame Agatha quite well. Ran
into her from time to time there."

"You also ran into Miss Lonsback at Durrants?"

"Yes. She was evaluating the hotel to see if she should recommend it to her clients. I believe I sold her on it. I was so enthusiastic I believe she suspected me of being a secret owner of the place. A charming young woman. Quite a shrewd mind for business, too. I gather you've developed a fondness for Miss Lonsback that goes beyond a business project."

Morgan chuckled. "Who's the detective in this room, Sir Malcolm?"

"One doesn't have to be Sherlock Holmes to recognize the obvious, Mr. Morgan."

25
The Five Orange Pips

As a Wellington mantel clock chimed eight, the guests of Sir Malcolm Bannister sat for dinner. A long table gleaming with silver service and blue and white Minton plates stood before an ornately carved wood and marble fireplace decorated with the clock, Copeland vases, Stevenson and Hancock porcelain figures of chubby youths, and modeled ceramic figures of various breeds of dogs. "This is a marvelous evocation of the Victorian era," said Wiggins, seated at one end of the table opposite Sir Malcolm. "My congratulations."

"I was torn between reproducing the dining hall in the style of sixteenth-century Sir Hugo Baskerville or the more resplendent and comfortable Victorian of Sir Henry Baskerville. I chose Sir Henry because that was the style which greeted Holmes and Watson when they came to investigate the mystery of the moor."

"Excuse me, Sir Malcolm." The servant approached the head of the table, a silver tray in his hand.

"What is it, Alexander?"

"These are for your guests, sir," said the young man as he held the tray in front of Sir Malcolm. Upon it lay a pile of white envelopes.

"Curious," said Sir Malcolm.

"What is it?" asked Morgan.

"Five envelopes. Each one addressed to a Man of Tor."

"Well, let's have them," said Wiggins enthusiastically. "Pass them along, Sir Malcolm."

"Is there anyone at this table who doesn't have an idea what's in them?" asked Benjamin Artnikoff, grimly.

"I don't," said Carrie Lonsback. Her face was a mixture of puzzlement and worry.

"Then let us see," said Artnikoff, tearing open the envelope. Shaking it, he held his palm beneath the opening.

Into his hand tumbled five orange seeds.

"The Five Orange Pips," gasped Bill Miner.

"A warning of death," Cliff Brownglass said.

"Alexander, where did you get these envelopes?" asked Morgan.

"I found them on the table in the great hall a few moments ago. I have no idea how they got there, sir.

They were not there half an hour ago. It would have been quite easy for someone to come in the front door, however, and leave them. The staff have been quite busy preparing for dinner, sir."

"Thank you, Alexander. You may leave us," said Sir Malcolm. He waited until the servant left and closed the huge doors. "This is a very disturbing turn of events. I'm at a loss . . ."

"It seems as if our murderer has followed us to Baskerville Hall," said Wiggins as he toyed with the five orange seeds from his own envelope. "Or came here with us." Wiggins rolled his great head and glanced at each of the Men of Tor. When his eyes turned to Morgan he asked, "Now do you believe it's one of us, Morgan?"

"It's possible," Morgan said hesitantly.

"David, that's horrible," said Carrie Lonsback.

"At the moment I have no choice but to suspect everyone."

"These are your friends."

"These are also very clever men who are well-versed in the theory, if not the practice, of murder. Clearly, the person who is sending these envelopes with their hints of danger is an accomplished Sherlockian. Around this table are some of the most prominent men in the circle of Holmesiana. It would come as no surprise to anyone here to learn that there are ample motives for murder in this room. Ben, when I asked you if there were any reasons why I shouldn't suspect you, what was your answer?"

"I said there was no reason."

"But you were joking, of course," said Carrie Lonsback.

"Not at all. I'm human and therefore capable of anything human. There's nothing more human than murder. Morgan ought to regard me as a suspect. He ought
to suspect all of us."

Morgan turned to Bill Miner. "You have reason to
suspect Jimmy Cape."

James Donald Cape laughed. "Really? For what reason?"

"Bill's collection of *Strand* magazines."

"Yes, I hadn't thought of that but, of course, a complete set of *The Strand*, some of which are signed
by Conan Doyle, would be very tempting. But how
would I obtain them even if I were to murder dear old
Bill?"

"Bill's son would happily sell them to you," said Morgan.

"Really? I'll keep that in mind," said James Donald
Cape.

"This isn't funny," snapped Carric Lonsback.

"Why suspect me?" asked Cliff Brownglass.

"Oh, the television deal that went sour because of
Ethan Remarque who is now dead. You had motive,
means, and opportunity, after all."

"If I granted you that I had motive and means, when
did I have the opportunity?"

"When you went up to Ethan's room to see why he
hadn't joined us in the dining room at Durrants Hotel."

"Ethan's room was locked."

"The hall porter had an extra key. It's quite easy to
take a key from the little pigeon holes when the hall
porter is distracted or away from his desk. And just as
easy to return it. Simply drop it in the box."

"Anyone could have done that."

"Yes. And I believe someone did just that to gain entry to Ethan's room."

"But Scotland Yard says it was a death by natural causes," said Cliff Brownglass.

"It wasn't, I assure you. Ethan was poisoned. A lethal dose of a drug administered by hypodermic needle. It might have been the kind you use, Cliff, for your own injections of insulin."

Cliff Brownglass smiled. "Say, I am rather a ripe suspect, aren't I?"

"As you said, anyone could have obtained a key to Ethan's room during the several hours that afternoon when Carrie and I were out of the hotel. All of you were there, each one of you alone. Any of the Men of Tor could have slipped into Ethan's room."

"You must now account for the murder of Herman Sloan," suggested Wiggins. "Herm was shot several miles from Manhattan. It would have taken quite a bit of doing for one of us to shoot Herman and arrive at the Queen Victoria hotel in time for the Irregulars dinner."

"Not at all. The killer easily could have boarded the very train that Herman was bicycling to catch. The distance and time are not factors at all, you see."

"But the attack on me, how do you account for that?"

"There is one point of interest in that attack, Wiggy. You were the only witness to it. You could have made up the whole thing as a cover for your own murderous activities in connection with Herm Sloan. Your motive, of course, was your hostility to Sir Malcolm's Sherlockian project. Or the tiff you had with Ben Artnikoff. Oh, you are a very serious contender in the suspects department, my friend."

Wiggins laughed. "I love it. How about Bill Miner?"

"Bill is like the dog that did nothing in the nighttime. I have found no reason to suspect him, so that makes him suspect above all."

"This is outrageous, Morgan," growled Bill Miner.

"Ah, he doth protest too much," said Ben Artnikoff.

Sir Malcolm Bannister, his lean face wreathed in amusement, asked, "Might I qualify? After all, it is I who invited you all to Baskerville Hall. In the literature of the English country house mystery the host always ranks high on the list of suspects."

"That's very generous of you, Sir Malcolm," said Morgan with a nod. "Thank you for saying so. I feel less guilty at having had you on my list from the very beginning."

"And what about you, Morgan?" Ben Artnikoff asked. "There've been plenty of yarns in which the detective turned out to be the villain."

"No," said Wiggins. "Morgan was not on the list of persons coming to visit Sir Malcolm. Even if we assume Morgan had motive and means, he lacked opportunity."

"He's told us himself how easily the murder of Herman Sloan could have been done," suggested Bill Miner.

"But the attack on me took place minutes before I arrived at his apartment," argued Wiggins.

"You were attacked by two men. Hirelings," replied Bill Miner.

"And you leave unexplained how Morgan could expect to murder us one by one during a trip to England which did not include him."

"Morgan deduced that you would invite him to come along, as you did," said Cliff Brownglass.

"I'll take that as a compliment," Morgan said.

Wiggins drummed his fingertips on the arm of his huge chair. "This is delicious. What a pack of suspicious characters we are."

"How about me?" asked Carrie Lonsback. "Am I to be left out of this morbid little game?"

Morgan lifted her hand and kissed it. "My chivalrous instincts impell me to dismiss you as a possibility . . ."

"Just because I'm a woman?"

"Oh, no. Hear me out. I said that my instincts as a gentleman impell me in that direction but anything gentlemanly about me is invariably overwhelmed by the cynical and suspicious nature that made me a detective in the first place. The fact that you're a woman wouldn't exclude you as a suspect. One must never forget that one of of the most winning women Sherlock Holmes ever knew poisoned her children for the insurance money. No, Carrie, I discount you simply because you have no motive."

"Thank you very much."

Wiggins clucked his tongue. "I think you're in trouble, Morgan, just when things were going so well for you."

"I beg your pardon?"

"Oh, Morgan, the only subject as interesting to the Men of Tor as this murderous plot against us has been the obviously blossoming romance between the two of you."

"That's ridiculous."

"You have been rather blatant about it, Morgan," said Ben Artnikoff. He turned to Carrie Lonsback solicitously. "I'm sorry if we've embarassed you, my dear. We're unrepentant gossips."

"An interest in the scandals, romances, and gossip

of the day has always been the hallmark of the true Sherlockian," said Wiggins. "Holmes himself cared nothing about the contents of newspapers except the crime news, the society notes, and the agony column."

"As a Sherlockian, Morgan is certain to break your heart," Ben Artnikoff said.

"Take our advice, my dear Miss Lonsback," said Wiggins, "and shun him like the plague."

26
The Noble Bachelor

After dinner while the Men of Tor and Sir Malcolm Bannister gathered in the drawing room of Baskerville Hall to discuss business over cigars and brandy, David Morgan and Carrie Lonsback settled into a carved and gilt Louis XIV sofa in the library. She stroked the lush upholstery. "Do you think this is genuine or a reproduction?"

"Sir Malcolm strikes me as a man who would not even look at reproductions."

"I can't begin to imagine being as rich as Sir Malcolm."

"Would you want to be?"

"Why not?"

"Well, Sir Malcolm is a bachelor. Why don't you marry him?"

She tossed her long blond hair. "He hasn't asked me to."

"How come you haven't married?"

"How come you haven't?"

"Do you really care?"

She stared at the flames licking a huge log in the fireplace. "Of course I care."

Morgan circled her slender shoulder with an arm. "Apparently you and I have provided a good deal of amusement for the others. Wiggy's right. Men are terrible gossips. I suppose we've been talked about quite a lot by the Men of Tor."

She smiled. "We're an item, all right."

"Does that please you?"

"It amuses me. How about you?"

"I ought to reply with a Sherlockianism."

"I'd prefer a Morganism."

"Carrie, I'm a man on the rebound. There's a woman I've been involved with. Name's Nicole Varney. It appears to be over, however."

"Sorry."

"Being on the rebound, I'm not sure you ought to trust me or to put any credence into what I might say."

"I'm a big girl now."

"We're both grown-ups and ought to act grown-up. If we were to apply some Sherlockian deduction to our situation—"

"Leave Sherlock Holmes out of it, please."

"Hear me through, Carrie. Be logical, okay? I'm considerably older than you. My line of work is not exactly the most stable means of earning a living. I have the classic male vices. I smoke too much, drink far too much, stay out all night, hang around with disreputable characters, and I have never been able to make a genuine commitment to a woman in my life. Don't misunderstand. I adore women. I've had quite a few in my time. But when they start getting serious I start getting the jitters. The slightest hint of wedding bells turns me into a first-class coward. My palms sweat and, like that black chauffeur in the Charlie Chan movies, I look down at my shoes and say, 'Feets, do yo' stuff.' That is not exactly the kind of guy who ought to be in the company of an upright girl who went to the proper schools, who reads real literature instead of detective novels, and who's got a travel business to run. In short, there is nothing about me that should interest you in the least."

"That's very noble, Mr. Morgan, but you overlook one small fact."

"And what is this small fact that I've missed?"

"I love you."

"Carrie, I . . ."

She lifted one of his hands and laughed. "Sweaty."

"I told you, I—" She cut him off with a kiss. When he opened his eyes he whispered, "This was not supposed to happen."

"It has happened."

Morgan drew away. "I shouldn't've let it happen."

"I'm quite prepared to forgive you all the little sins you outlined a moment ago. I have a few foibles of my own."

"This case is complicated already. I hate complications."

"What have our feelings for each other got to do with this case?"

Morgan shrugged. "Holmes says a true reasoner, a detective, must be single-minded. He never permitted affairs of the heart—women—to get in his way."

"Was Holmes a queer?"

Morgan laughed. "Just because two men share an apartment . . ."

Carrie slipped a hand into his. "Obviously, you'll have to hurry up and solve this case. I don't care for complications either, and this case is complicating whatever it is that's happening between us."

"Is something happening?"

"You know there is."

"Yes, I do."

"Very well, then you'll have to find the murderer as soon as possible. I believe you can eliminate all the other suspects and concentrate on the ones here at Baskerville Hall. The critic, the producer, the man named Bell, all seem like long shots to me."

Amused, Morgan asked, "When did you become a detective?"

"A woman can't be a detective?"

"Okay, you tell me your choice for the murderer."

"What about Sir Malcolm?"

"That's a rude way to treat your host and future business partner, Carrie."

She made a face, thinking. "Yes. You ought to eliminate Sir Malcolm as a suspect. He's much too nice to be a killer."

Laughing, Morgan hugged her. "If it were up to you there wouldn't be any suspects left."

"I see your point. I leave the solution of these murders entirely up to you."

27
The Man on Tor

While the occupants of Baskerville Hall slept, Morgan sat by the window of his bedroom smoking a pipe and staring out at the broad dark sweep of the moor rolling away from the front of the hall toward the craggy black silhouette of Tor. Below the window, trees moaned and swung in the wind and Morgan half expected to hear the distant howl of the Hound. It had been several hours since the last of the Men of Tor closed his bedroom door and locked it from inside and Morgan had come to his own room to wait. Dawn was only a suggestion in a thin pale-red line between the heavy overcast and the deep black ridge of the moor sloping away from Tor, when Morgan heard the quiet tap upon his door. "Come in, Alex."

"I've spotted the signal, sir," said the young man as he poked his head into the room.

"Is everything quiet in the house?"

"Not a creature is stirring, sir, except us. And the man on the moor."

Morgan stood and put on a heavy coat. "Must have been damned cold out there tonight."

"The wind's up. We may be having some snow by morning."

Morgan glanced out the window. The moor was a

mixture of black shadows and long fingers of reddish dawn poking among the crags. "Let's go then."

Over the wide expanse of the moor there was no sound but the moan of the cold wind and no movement except the two figures bundled in heavy coats as they trudged upon crisply frosted grass and hardened mud toward the rugged silhouette of Tor. Presently, Morgan saw movement in the gray light near the rocky foot of Tor as the sun rose behind the overcast. A few moments later, Chief Superintendent Ivor Griffith held out a gloved hand. "Welcome to Dartmoor." He flashed a smile and looked across the desolate sweep of the moor. "Hardly a place for camping, eh? How are things at Baskerville Hall?" He barked a laugh through a gust of steam. "Any sign of the hound of Hell, Morgan?"

"All's quiet so far. Young Alexander, here, has been just fine."

The chief superintendent winked at Alexander. "Well, I always said Alex ought to have been an actor instead of a policeman. There's always a need for types to play the faithful butler, eh, Alex? There's a little hollow in the rocks over there where I've been waiting. I've got a thermos."

An outcropping of black granite shielded them from the wind as Griffith poured coffee into paper cups. "Have you gotten a line on Westin and Hess-Feldstein?"

Griffith sipped noisily. "Strike them from your list, Morgan. Westin has an ironclad alibi for the hour when Remarque was murdered. Mr. Westin was in conference with none other than His Royal Highness, the Prince of Wales. A meeting concerning a TV documentary which His Royal Highness is giving his backing to.

One of those nature things the BBC does so well and so repeatedly. Hess-Feldstein moved on. He was in Paris."

"So we are left with the Men of Tor themselves."

"You're not surprised?"

"No. Disappointed."

"I trust that no new corpses have been discovered?"

"Alexander kept an eye on everyone during the night."

"Excellent. Suppose you hightail it back to the hall now, Alex. Wouldn't want another murder while we're here drinking this appallingly bad coffee, eh?"

"No, sir," said the young man.

Morgan and Griffith watched as Alexander sprinted across the moor toward the gray sprawl of Baskerville Hall. "He really is quite good in the role of butler, Ivor. If you're not careful, Sir Malcolm might make him a better offer than the Yard could manage, given the austerity budget you fellows are operating on."

"Now that we've eliminated Westin and Hess-Feldstein, I believe it's time for Scotland Yard to take over this case, Morgan."

"Ivor, we agreed on how to proceed. You've got your man in the hall. Your men are only a few minutes away in the village. Trust me, Ivor. I'm very close. Very close."

"It's damned irregular."

"That is a very grim pun, Ivor."

Light snow began falling as Morgan made his way toward Baskerville Hall but soon flakes became stinging pellets driven by a biting wind that blew the snow into a veil to obscure the rooftops and turrets of the hall. "We appear to be in for quite a blow, Morgan,"

said the tall and slender man bending into the wind. "You and your friends may find yourselves snowed in."

"Charming."

"The classic setting for a murder mystery. The closed environment of an English manor house, a small group of persons who know each other, and who also know that one of them is a murderer. I shall look forward to the moment when you gather the suspects together in the drawing room and unmask the villain of the piece. You've even arranged for a Scotland Yard man to be at hand, discreetly off-stage awaiting his cue. I can hear you now. 'Chief Superintendent, here is your man!' Sheer melodrama, Morgan."

"I'm glad to note that you've decided to come to Baskerville Hall to lend your moral support if not your help."

"Why, you need no help, Morgan. You're doing splendidly. The orange pips were an amusing touch. Was the ploy instructive?"

"I picked up a few interesting points. Small ones."

"Watch for the small things. You'll recall that in the dreadful business of the Abernetty family of Baltimore it was my noticing of the depth to which the parsley had sunk into the butter on a warm day which gave me my first clue."

"Thank you for the reminder."

The pungent aroma of wood burning in fireplaces mixed with the snow slanting into Morgan's face as he trudged off the moor, crossed a narrow road piling high at the sides with drifting snow, and entered the wide courtyard in front of the hall. A gust of wind whipped snow into crystaline vortexes and the smell of fires was spiced with the fragrance of breakfast sausages being cooked.

Morgan saw the muzzle flash, heard the bark of the weapon, and thought he felt the snap of the bullet as it whizzed past his ear. Then he was aware only of the cold wet snow under him as he sprawled on his belly and waited for a second shot. When it did not come, he pushed himself up and ran for the door of Baskerville Hall. Inside, Alexander rushed to help him with his coat. "You're covered with snow, sir. Did you slip and fall?"

Morgan shook melting snow from his hands and stomped his feet. "Somebody just took a potshot at me."

"Christ," grunted Alexander, reaching for the door.

"No use going out. He's gone. Fired one shot from a clump of trees. With the snow and the wind, his tracks will be obliterated. Where is everyone?"

"Sir Malcolm and the others are having breakfast in the dining hall. Except for Mr. Cape. I believe he's still asleep."

"Go and have a look, Alex. And not a word about this to anyone."

"Yes, sir."

Around the table sat Sir Malcolm, Carrie Lonsback, Wiggins, Ben Artnikoff, Bill Miner, and Cliff Brownglass. Sir Malcolm stood, a worried look on his face. "Lord, have you been out in this beastly storm, Mr. Morgan?"

"A little morning constitutional, is all."

"My word. You look positively frozen. Have some coffee. Sit here by me."

Wiggins looked up from a plate of sausage and eggs.

"You'll note that we appear to have gotten through the night without any murders."

Carrie Lonsback made a face. "That isn't funny."

"No," Wiggins agreed, "but it is reassuring."

"Jimmy Cape's not here," Morgan noted. "Has anyone seen him this morning?"

"Jimmy's been up for some time," replied Bill Miner, buttering a triangle of toast. "He said he was going riding."

"Riding? In this gale?"

"It wasn't snowing when he went out. Said he was going to try Silver Blaze."

"I don't like it," Morgan said.

At that moment, Alexander appeared. "Mr. Cape's not in his room, sir."

"No, the bloody fool's gone horseback riding," said Ben Artnikoff.

Morgan stood. "Alexander, show me where the stables are, please."

"Relax," said Wiggins. "Jimmy's a big boy. He knows horses. He'll be back soon, I assure you. Besides, since we're all here in this room, nothing can happen to him. Have some bangers, David, and relax."

Morgan strode from the room. "All of you stay where you are until I get back."

28
Silver Blaze

The harness room smelled of leather and saddle soap. Silver bridle buckles reflected light from a single lamp at the center of a heavy oak table where the young blond American who had driven Morgan's four-wheeler bent over a pair of black leather riding boots. Startled, he looked up as Morgan barged in. "Morning, sir." He looked down and directed a droplet of saliva onto the toe of the boot. Scooping a gob of black polish onto his fingertips, he applied the polish and the spit in small circles. "Hope you weren't thinking of riding, sir. Hell of a snowstorm building out there."

"How long has Mr. Cape been out on Silver Blaze?"

"Better part of an hour, sir."

"Aren't you worried?"

"Worried, sir?"

"Yes, worried. Sir Malcolm's prize thoroughbred out in weather like this?"

"I expect they'll be back any minute. Blaze is a reliable animal. And I understand Mr. Cape is an expert horseman. No, I'm not worried."

"Well, dammit, I am, so saddle up two horses and do it now."

"Two, sir?"

"One for me and one for Alexander."

"I'd have to okay that with Sir Malcolm, sir."

"You'll do what I tell you to do or you'll be looking for a new job, I guarantee you. This is life and death, kid."

"Life and death?"

"So saddle two goddamned horses and do it now."

"Yes, sir. Whatever you say, sir."

"Which way did Mr. Cape go when he went out on Silver Blaze?"

"Right up the main trail, sir. I'll show you the way soon's I get you your mounts."

Morgan turned to Alexander. "You *do* ride, Alex?"

"I'm not Grand National class, but I manage to stay on."

"I hope and pray I'm wrong, Alex. God, how I hope and pray."

"I don't really understand why you're so upset."

"I'm upset because I'm a perfect jackass. I'm supposed to be preventing murders but I may have let another one happen right under my nose. And what a goddamned fool Jimmy Cape was to leave himself wide open like this. The son of a bitch should have stayed in the house. But no. He decides to go out for a ride on Silver Blaze. Christ, he may have played right into the murderer's hands."

"You've left me behind, Mr. Morgan."

"In the story *Silver Blaze* a man named Straker is killed. Stomped to death by the horse. Our murderer is inspired by the methods of death in the Holmes cases. A bullet in *The Solitary Cyclist.* Poison in *The Speckled Band.* Sticks in *The Illustrious Client.* Now we have *Silver Blaze.* Hurry the hell up, kid, with our horses."

"Coming, sir." A moment later he led the horses out of the barn. Holding them as Morgan and Alexander mounted, he nodded toward a distant gate. "That's the trail he took, sir."

Morgan's bay bent its head into the wind-blown snow and plodded gamely up a long sloping trail toward a charcoal gray stand of woods. Alexander's mottled gray seemed to dance with delight in the swirl. The trail curved into the woods to cut a long dark tunnel through stolid trees which blocked the wind and snow. "We'll probably meet Mr. Cape coming the other way," said Alexander.

"I hope so."

"He may have taken refuge at one of the nearby houses."

"Jimmy Cape has never taken refuge anywhere, Alex. No. Either we meet him coming back along this trail or . . ."

"What is it?"

"Up ahead. Coming toward us."

Alexander saw the horse as Morgan spoke. "Silver Blaze. But where's Mr. Cape?"

Morgan galloped ahead and caught Silver Blaze's bridle. Alexander trotted up behind. "The animal's quite wet. Cold. Been in the snow." Morgan peered through the dim forest tunnel toward gray light where the woods ended and the trail dipped into a snow-white valley. "No telling how far ahead on this trail we'll find him."

"He may have been thrown and is walking back."

"Jimmy Cape hasn't been thrown from a horse since he was three years old. C'mon, Alex." Holding Silver Blaze's reins, Morgan urged his bay forward. Five minutes later he spotted James Donald Cape's body curled at the side of the trail, a dusting of snow like powdered

sugar on the broad back and wide shoulders. Beneath
the crushed head a pool of blood had begun to freeze.
Morgan knelt in the inch-deep snow to study the
wounds. "Deep, deep gashes. As if he'd been clubbed
with a tire iron."

"Or a horse's hooves?"

"That's what it's supposed to look like, Alex."

"Something might have spooked Silver Blaze . . ."

"Alex, you're a policeman. Look at the evidence, the
pattern to these killings. Jimmy was a master at handling horses. He was clubbed to death by human hands
not a horse's hooves. Damn this snow! The tracks are
covered. If it weren't for this goddamned snow we'd
find plenty of evidence to show that I'm right. Jimmy
riding along here on Silver Blaze. Another rider, probably, coming up behind him or from the front. They
stop. Probably chat amicably. Someone Jimmy knew,
perhaps. Trusted. Then the murder. Carefully planned
to make it look like the death in the story." Morgan
stood and looked down at the body lying beneath the
shroud of snow. "And I let it happen. Christ, I am a fool.
I'm as guilty of these crimes as the madman who's com-
mitting them."

"Chief Superintendent Griffith will insist on taking
over completely, Mr. Morgan."

Morgan nodded. "Perhaps he should. Perhaps he
should have taken over in London."

"Well, we know now that no one at Baskerville Hall
is the murderer. None of them could have done this.
Not without help."

"You are exactly right, Alex. As the sleuth of Baker
Street put it, 'When a fact appears to be opposed to a
long train of deductions it invariably proves to be capa-

ble of bearing some other interpretation.' I've been looking at this case from the wrong end. I know, now, who our Moriarty is."

"You do?"

"Yes, and if you'll hightail it into the village and round up the rest of the Scotland Yarders and bring them to Baskerville Hall I'll hand over the killer to you."

"But Chief Inspector Griffith is—"

"There's no time, Alex. Get out of here. I'm going back to Baskerville Hall."

29

The Dying Detective

"The faculty of deduction is certainly contagious, Morgan."

"I've been blind as a bat."

"Indeed."

"*You* were misled on several occasions, as I recall."

"Yes. In *The Speckled Band* I had come to an entirely erroneous conclusion, which shows, my dear Morgan, how dangerous it is to reason from insufficient data. Now what do you propose to do?"

"I do not *propose* to do anything. I *intend* to identify the murderer."

"Be careful, Morgan. You have never been in greater danger."

Gamely, two horses plodded through the rapidly deepening snow as the storm mounted in fury. A fierce wind drove the snow horizontally, the tiny white pellets stinging like buckshot as Morgan's bay and Silver Blaze approached the gaping black mouth of the tunnel through the wintry woods. The snow crusted Morgan's cap and formed white epaulets on his shoulders. His face, although wet from the snow, burned as if he had spent too many hours under a Caribbean sun. The flush of excitement and the warmth of the knowledge of how the murders had been committed and who had been masterminding them surged through his body as the bay horse strove toward the momentary shelter of the woods. Silver Blaze, struggling behind, wheezed noisily into the hard wind. As the horses reached the crest of the hill and approached the mouth of the tunnel, they began to prance as if they were nearing their barn and a feeding-trough filled with oats. "We're almost there," Morgan muttered.

A few yards into the tunnel the shot rang out.

The bullet slammed into Morgan's right shoulder. Bone splintered. He both felt and heard it snap. The bullet's path bore into him like a dentist's drill. He did not know if the bullet had exploded out through his back. He knew only pain in his shoulder and chest and that he was being catapulted backward off his horse and toward the ground. An instant later he was on his back, awake, staring up at the dark canopy of leafless tree limbs, aware of the pain in his right shoulder and side, conscious of a wet spot spreading through his clothing from his collar bone to his belt on the right side, and a sticky wetness that made his clothing adhere to his back. He heard the whinny of the horses and the thudding of their hooves as they bolted. Then he heard only the wind. As he closed his eyes and surrendered to the dark, warm, wet, downward pull of a force outside himself he thought he heard the baleful howling of a animal —a wolf perhaps. No, he thought as he drifted deep into blackness, it's not a wolf. It's a hound. The Hound of the Baskervilles. Out on the moor. Baying in triumph.

He supposed he was dying.

30
The Dancing Men

The Hound of the Baskervilles was licking his face. In great, wet, sloppy strokes its immense tongue was coursing over him. Odd, he thought, that this fearsome spectral hound would lick him, tickle him, and not sink its vicious fangs into his throat to rip it out. Then he remembered something about lions. How lions lick their prey before devouring it. He was being licked by lions not the Hound. "No. No. No."

"It's all right. You're going to be all right."

Morgan opened his eyes to the face of Carrie Lonsback, half-smiling, half-worried. "It's you."

"Yes, it's Carrie. Don't move." She pressed a damp
cloth against his forehead then patted his cheek and
under his chin.

"I thought it was the Hound," he muttered. Behind
her, fuzzily, Morgan recognized other faces—Sir Malcolm, Ben Artnikoff, Cliff Brownglass, Wiggins. Their
faces loomed, dodged, drew near, drew away—like
dancing men. "How did I . . .?"

Sir Malcolm Bannister bent over him. "Don't try to
move. You have a broken shoulder. I've done my best.
Taped you up. I've given you something to ease the
pain. It was a small caliber bullet. A little larger
and . . ."

"Did you find Jimmy Cape? He's out there. Someone
should go and get him."

"We're having a blizzard. We can't look for him until
the snow stops."

"Have the police come?"

"No one can get through the storm," said Sir Malcolm. "I had a telephone call from the village. They will
be here as soon as possible."

"You spoke with Chief Superintendent Griffith?"

"No. One of his men. He said that until the chief
superintendent arrives none of us is to leave Baskerville
Hall, which seems a trifle superfluous considering the
weather. I gathered from the urgency in the young
man's voice that a breakthrough has occurred."

Morgan nodded. "Yes."

Wiggins stepped forward, his pumpkin face looming
over the bed. "Do you mean you've discovered the
identity of the murderer?"

"Yes."

Bill Miner appeared. "Is it one of us?"

Morgan closed his eyes.

"How often have I said to you that when you have eliminated the impossible, whatever remains, however improbable, must be the truth?"

"God, you can be insufferably smug sometimes."

"Yes. It is one of my more endearing qualities. The man asked you a question. How will you answer him?"

"I'm trying to decide how to answer."

"You may name the murderer, Morgan, but where is your evidence? What proof do you have that will hold up in a court of law? Deductive reasoning is not sufficient to persuade a jury. You need proof. Better yet, a confession. That would be a brilliant achievement, wouldn't it?"

"And you were the one who accused me of melodrama."

"Surely our profession would be a drab one if we did not sometimes set the scene so as to glorify our results."

"So you've said."

"What shall you do?"

"I shall sleep a little, I think."

Carrie Lonsback whispered, "He's asleep."

"It's the anesthetic I gave him," said Sir Malcolm. "We must leave him."

Wiggins shook his great head. "If we leave him alone he'll be in grave danger."

"We shan't leave him alone. We men will leave. Miss

Lonsback will stay with him. We will go down to the drawing room and remain together until Chief Superintendent Griffith arrives."

"And what about the person who shot him? Suppose whoever fired that shot in the woods comes here looking for him?"

"Miss Lonsback will have this to keep her company," said Sir Malcolm, handing her a revolver.

31
A Case of Identity

Morgan opened his eyes. "So, we're alone."

"They couldn't make up their minds about whom they ought to trust to watch over you."

"Gentlemanly of them to choose you."

"Yes."

"A dreadful mistake, of course."

"I'm afraid so." She stood just out of reach of his bed. "How did you know?"

"Little things. Those little slips of the tongue, lapses of thought, inconsequential bits and pieces. Trifles. Do you really want to know?"

"Of course I do." Smiling, she sat. The revolver pointed at Morgan's chest. "David, I couldn't kill you without knowing what you know. I'd lie awake nights wondering."

"They'll come back if you use that gun."

"It has six bullets. And I am a terrific shot."

"Your brother's not so bad, either."

"Oh, you are good, Morgan. Actually, both my brothers are experts with a rifle."

"Just so I won't have any sleepless nights, later, which one of them shot Herman Sloan?"

"My older brother. Kevin."

"Then the fellow who shot me was . . ."

"Lex."

"Is Kevin also a blond?"

"Kevin has brunette hair. Lex and I are the blonds. We got our hair from our mother. Kevin took after our father."

"Joseph Bell."

"Yes."

"It's not easy working under an alias, but yours was quite a good one. I don't care much for puns or plays on words, but Carrie Lonsback is excellent. Carrielon's-back. Carillon's back. Bell's back. Nifty. I didn't figure that out until a few minutes ago, actually. The rest of it came together somewhat sooner. Of course, I made the mistake of allowing emotion to get in the way of pure logic."

"A fatal mistake, David. Too bad. You know your Canon but you don't always live by it. That's what they call sin, you know."

"May I go through it step by step? You may feel free to make any corrections."

"It ought to be fascinating."

"Obviously, I knew I was dealing with someone who was an expert on Holmes. The Men of Tor are the acknowledged experts in the cult of Sherlockiana but my nemesis was a far better Sherlockian than any of the

Men of Tor. You did very well playing the role of someone who claimed to be virtually ignorant of the Canon
but you slipped from time to time. It's natural. No true
Sherlockian can avoid letting the Sacred Writings seep
into the little moments of life. We all quote Holmes or
Watson all the time, even if the person listening is not
aware of it. You told me that you were not 'into'
Holmes. But when we were on Baker Street and I was
waxing poetic about 221–B you asked me how many
steps there were to Holmes's rooms. I answered cor-
rectly. Seventeen. I could have answered sixteen or
twenty or a hundred and two and it wouldn't've mat-
tered. Only the genuine Sherlockian appreciates that
Holmes made a point of counting the number of steps
and then testing Watson. That you *asked* the question
was significant."

"Yes, I recognized that error immediately."

"You also referred to the dog that remained silent in
the night. You knew that Holmes *cabled* Wilson Hargreave of the New York police. Pure Holmesian trivia,
Carrie."

"Carolyn."

"Yes. I was misled for a time—quite a long time,
actually—by the names of Joseph Bell's children. When
I spoke with my associate Kenny he said there were
three sons. Kevin, Lex, and Carl or Calvin. It took me
an unforgivably long time to realize that the third child
might be named Carla or Carolyn. It's shocking how
inattentive ordinary people can be. Your mother's
neighbors were terribly sloppy in either hearing the
name of the third child or recalling it for Kenny's benefit. Of course, the neighbors never actually met you."

"I was away at school a good deal of my life. My father

valued education for his daughter as much as he did for
his sons."

"The boys must have been a crushing disappointment. One becomes a drop-out. The other joins the
Marines. Lex was the Marine?"

"Yes. Both have redeemed themselves in my father's
eyes, however."

"Too bad he's too bonkers to know."

"*I* know." She smiled. "How did you know about my
brothers? I mean, how did you connect Carrie Lonsback to the fact of her having brothers?"

"You said that your father used to read to *us*. A small
slip, granted. Naturally, in addition to reading *The Pied
Piper of Hamlin* he would have read Sherlock Holmes
to his sons and to his tomboy."

"Every one of the novels and stories. Dad was a great
Sherlockian. He deserved to be a member of the Baker
Street Irregulars."

"That he wasn't admitted must have been a blow, but
to let such a trivial thing eat at one's mind and to drive
one to madness?"

"My father was a tender and sensitive man. Your
friends treated him cruelly. I made up my mind to get
even. *Rache.*"

"Your scheme would make Professor Moriarty envi-
ous. It began when? A year or so ago when your father
finally went completely nuts?"

"Yes."

"Please correct me on any small points. It was, I believe, your brother Lex who provided the first inklings
of how you might go about getting revenge against the
Men of Tor. He was in the Marines and assigned to duty
at the United States Embassy in London?"

"Bravo, David."

"The embassy is on Grosvenor Square, not very far from Durrants Hotel. Lex runs into Sir Malcolm Bannister at the hotel and—"

"May I correct you?"

"Please do."

"Lex first encountered Sir Malcolm at an embassy reception and learned at that time that Sir Malcolm was a ranking member of the Sherlock Holmes Society of London. It was easy for him to determine where Sir Malcolm stayed when he came to London from Baskerville Hall."

"That's when you developed an interest in exploring Durrants Hotel. Not just as a possible hotel to recommend to the clients of the Lonsback Travel Agency but to plan one of the murders that were now taking shape in your mind along with the scheme to lure the Men of Tor to the hotel. You studied the hotel routines, its floor plan, its little quirks and idiosyncracies. That made it quite simple for your brother to obtain a key to Ethan Remarque's room and to murder him."

"May I fine-tune here a bit?"

"Be my guest."

"In addition to learning Durrants Hotel through and through, I managed to get my brother Kevin a job there as one of the bellmen. In fact, Kevin showed you to your room."

"Ah, that was Kevin. Very helpful. May I assume that it was Kevin who murdered Ethan?"

"While you were showing me the splendors of Baker Street."

"That's why you lured me away with your invitation to lunch."

"Exactly."

"Kevin had to do some smart traveling to fly from London to Long Island, shoot Herman Sloan in the back, and return to Durrants Hotel and his job."

"I *am* in the travel business, David."

"So you are. You've learned the job well in . . . how long?"

"The Lonsback Agency's been in business a year."

"You went to very great extremes to carry out your plot."

"It was worth it. As to Kevin's travels, the Concorde has made the trip to New York and back a matter of hours."

"I thought it might have been Kevin whom Ethan recognized at the hotel."

"Impossible."

"I wonder what he saw? What he wanted to tell me?"

"That is something neither you nor I will ever know. I assume he spotted the critic. Anything else on your mind?"

"The use of Thorazin to murder Ethan was a very important clue. It's a powerful sedative used in controlling mental patients, such as your father. There must have been plenty of times when you and your brothers had to use it on him."

"My father suffered, David."

"Who attacked Wiggins?"

"Kevin and Lex."

"If they hadn't botched it you might have succeeded in all this."

"But I have succeeded."

"You were quite good, Carrie. Superb, in fact. Only twice did your composure crack and nearly give you

away. During the offering of toasts at the Sherlock
Holmes pub you were taken aback when you suggested
toasting the real Sherlock Holmes, meaning Conan
Doyle, and Ben Artnikoff thought you meant Dr. Joseph Bell, Conan Doyle's real-life model for Holmes. It
had to have been an awful shock to hear your father's
name."

"It was. Especially in that setting. My father and I
dined in that very restaurant on a number of occasions.
During the last visit to the recreated study my father
broke down and wept because of the insult the Men of
Tor had handed him."

"You seemed a little shaken when Alexander brought
the orange pips to Sir Malcolm's dining hall."

"A cheap trick on your part, David."

"It didn't shake you?"

"Only for an instant. Then I was amused. Immediately I recognized what you were hoping for. That the
murderer who had sent the cards in New York would
be upset by the arrival of the pips, knowing that he—
I—hadn't sent them. That was when I knew you were
nowhere near solving the murders. I was terribly disappointed. Yet, here we are a few hours later and you
have the whole thing drawn together. How ever did
you do it?"

"When I found Jimmy Cape's body it was obvious
that his killer could not have been anyone from Baskerville Hall. There wasn't time. Well, I *knew* that the
murderer *was* one of the people at Baskerville Hall. Yet
here was a murder which no one at the hall could have
done. Alexander pointed that out to me. He's a Scotland
Yard detective, by the way. The murder of Jimmy Cape
was incontrovertible evidence that the murderer had

an accomplice and that accomplice was at Baskerville
Hall. I began to suspect an accomplice when someone
took a shot at me this morning while all of you were at
breakfast. Jimmy Cape was absent, and for a little while
there was the possibility he had taken that shot at me.
Finding him dead rather emphatically ruled him out as
a suspect, of course. Because all of you were here at the
hall, I had no other conclusion to draw except that
someone else was involved. That person had to be a
horseman. He had to know that Jimmy Cape was out
riding and what trail he took. He had to have great
strength to inflict the blows that killed Jimmy. Now,
whom did I know at Baskerville Hall who fit those qua-
lifications? The fellow who saw Jimmy Cape off on Silver Blaze. The same chap who handled Sir Malcolm's
horse team so well. The handsome blond American in
charge of Sir Malcolm's stables. Some of this began adding up when someone took that shot at me at breakfast
time. That shot indicated that I had become a threat.
It was the rash act of a frightened person, but the person I'd been trying to unmask has never been frightened. The person planning these murders would never
have permitted the attack on me. I assume that you
mentioned to your skittish brother that I was suspicious
of him and he panicked. Your means of neutralizing me
was far more subtle. Was it all an act or did you care for
me a little?"

"Under other circumstances you'd be quite appeal-
ing. But you were a complication. We both hate complications."

"Your brother's not as cool as you, unfortunately."

"He's impetuous."

"I was fooled for quite a while. I didn't come to my

senses until it was almost too late. It all fell into place
when Sir Malcolm was treating my wound. You and
your brothers will be arrested and tried for murder, of
course, no matter what happens to me."

"They can only hang me once."

"If you get yourself a smart lawyer you might be able
to pin everything on your brothers."

"*I* planned everything, David. They couldn't've
done anything without me."

"**I believe that amounts to a confession?**"

"**It does. However, if you're dead, who will testify
at their trial?**"

"**What about you?**"

"**Morgan, you are quite droll. Who would ever
believe me? To most of the world I have never been
anything but the figment of Sir Arthur Conan Doyle's
imagination. Besides which, the woman in question is
pointing a gun at you and, unless I am mistaken, has
every intention of shooting you. Don't count on her
recent demonstrations of affection. I would not underestimate her will to use that gun.**"

"**It isn't loaded.**"

"**Of course it's loaded. Why would Sir Malcolm
give her an unloaded weapon?**"

"**Really, my friend, has that legendary logic failed
you at last?**"

"**Yes, of course. I see your point. Obviously the
gun isn't loaded. Morgan, you are a revelation.**"

"**Really, Holmes, it was elementary.**"

"From a strictly intellectual view, your planning of
the murders was admirable, Carrie."

"Thank you, David."

"And your knowledge of the Canon puts the Men of Tor—and me—to shame. You'd make a splendid addition to the Baker Street Irregulars."

"Except that I'm a woman."

"To me, Carrie, you'll always be *the* woman. Next year when we toast Irene Adler I'll be thinking of you."

"Next year? David, I'm going to kill you. And the others."

"The pistol you hold in your hand isn't loaded, Carrie."

"God, you are amazing, David."

"If you don't believe me, pull the trigger."

With a shrug and a smile, she said, "Goodbye, David."

Click.

"I told you it wasn't loaded."

Click. Click. Click. Click.

"One more, Carrie."

Click.

"Morgan, you bastard."

"I'm sorry, Carrie. Truly. You're a great Sherlockian but so am I. You were superb at drawing on the Canon to carry out your crimes, but you never tumbled to the fact that I was using the Canon, also. In fact, I was afraid I was being obvious in taking a page from *The Hound of the Baskervilles.*"

"What are you talking about?"

"Did you really believe I'd come to Baskerville Hall and not make arrangements for my own Man on Tor?"

"I don't . . ."

"Chief Inspector Griffith. He's been outside the door to this room and has heard everything you've said, including your admission to the planning of the murders.'

"Griffith is in the village. The snow. The phone call."

"He sneaked into Baskerville Hall this morning while we were at breakfast. So even if you had succeeded in murdering me, he would have been on hand to place you under arrest. Which I think he may wish to do right now. Ivor?"

"Here," said Chief Superintendent Ivor Griffith as he stepped into the bedroom.

32

The Sign of Four

"In spite of all that has happened," said Sir Malcolm Bannister as he stood before the great fireplace in the library of Baskerville Hall, "I hope that our project has not been scuttled."

"Certainly not," exclaimed B. Alexander Wiggins from the comfort of an enormous late-Victorian chesterfield sofa. "All of us remain committed to the project."

"Here, here," said Benjamin Artnikoff, stroking his muttonchops.

"There is," suggested Bill Miner, "the added romance of the events which have taken place in this house."

"My God, you are crass," Cliff Brownglass said.

"If we agree to proceed, I'll have my solicitors draw up the documents," said Sir Malcolm, smiling. "When the papers are ready you fellows can have a little ceremony to sign them. And I hope you'll invite Mr. Morgan."

"The sign of the four?" Morgan asked.

"Of course, Mr. Morgan, if you'd care to become a partner?"

"No, thanks, Sir Malcolm. I've had my fill of the travel business."

"You got what was coming to you, Morgan," said Wiggins. "You brushed aside every lesson of the Canon concerning women."

"At the risk of sounding like one of my own novels," said Ben Artnikoff, stepping forward, "I must say that there is one thing that puzzles me, Morgan. Why did Sir Malcolm give Carrie an unloaded gun?"

"Elementary," Wiggins said.

"Indeed?"

"Morgan asked him to. Correct?"

"Yes."

Cliff Brownglass exploded. "When?"

"While Sir Malcolm was treating my wound and I was piecing together all the parts of the puzzle and coming to the unhappy but inescapable truth about Carrie Lonsback. Lying there, I was trying to find any deductive flaw to divert me from that conclusion. Sir Malcolm looked me square in the eyes and said, 'When you have excluded the impossible, whatever remains, however improbable, must be the truth.' I understood at that moment that Sir Malcolm had come to the same conclusion. Then it was simply a matter of working out a way to get Carrie to confess. Our plan involved Sir Malcolm ordering everyone to leave me alone *except* Carrie, to whom he would give the unloaded pistol, and stationing Chief Superintendent Griffith outside the door."

"The subtle trap," muttered Chief Superintendent Griffith from the shadows in a corner of the library.

"Three cheers for the man from Scotland Yard." Morgan laughed.

Frowning, Chief Superintendent Griffith said, "That's a pleasant switch."

33

Train From Waterloo

Morgan looked up at the board listing the arrivals and departures of trains in the vast echoing concourse of Waterloo Station. He sought out one sign in particular.

SOUTHHAMPTON DOCKS
BOAT TRAIN
CUNARD LINE

"Kind of romantic, isn't it?" he asked, glancing at Chief Superintendent Ivor Griffith.

Griffith shook his head. "It's no wonder you're a Sherlockian. The commonest things take on meaning. You look a little romantic yourself with your arm in a sling. Except for that you look none the worse for wear for your visit to England. Unless there's damage elsewhere? The heart, for instance?"

"My heart is my least vulnerable part, Ivor."

"Did you really fall for her, or was that an act put on by the unrelenting detective out to get his man, or, in this case, his woman."

"*The* woman. Holmes has Irene Adler. I have Carrie Lonsback, a.k.a. Carolyn Bell. A brilliant woman, Ivor. I felt really bad looking at her in the dock at Old Bailey."

"If she'd shown even the slightest remorse she might have fared a little better in the sentencing. There's nothing a British judge likes more than to show a merciful heart when he hands down a sentence. The slightest flicker of repentence can knock off a few years."

Morgan stared at the sign. "It would have been totally out of character. Pride is a powerful emotion, Ivor. That's what this was about. Pride. I think if she could have paraded her pride and humiliated the Men of Tor in some other way she wouldn't've turned to murder."

"You did love her."

Morgan looked down. "You bet."

The boat train eased from its berth at Waterloo Station and rolled southwesterly, rumbling through Lambeth and Vauxhall and picking up speed as Morgan leaned back in the seat of his first class compartment, alone. A soft London rain streaked the window. Morgan did not look up when the door of the compartment opened and closed and a tall gentleman sat down opposite him.

"I understand for the first time how you felt when you brought a case to a satisfactory conclusion and suddenly had nothing to do," Morgan said.

"Hence the cocaine."

"I'll pass."

"What is the use of having powers, Morgan, when one has no field upon which to exert them? My life has been spent in one long effort to escape from the commonplaces of existence. I think I may go so far as to say that I have not lived in vain. The air of London is sweeter for my presence. In over a thousand cases I am not aware that I have ever used my powers upon the wrong side. Now I'm afraid time and the science of criminology have passed me by. What I used to achieve with my methods is done these days with computers and forensic science. It's all for the best, of course, but I do feel sorry for the policemen of today. There's not much room for intuition, deduction, and reason. I'm an anachronism, I fear. As out of date as the four-wheeler, the gasogene, the magnifying glass, and the high silk hat. I am a relic, Morgan."

"That's not true."

"Ah, but it is."

"You'll never be out of date. Not as long as some ten-year-old somewhere can wander into the stacks of a library and take down one of Watson's stories and spend an hour, an afternoon, a day, an evening—a lifetime—with you."

The tall man with the hawkish nose took out the pipe, lit it, puffed a swirling cloud of smoke, and al-

lowed himself a slight smile. "Good old Watson. I
would be lost without my Boswell." He stood and
pulled open the door. Stepping into the corridor, he
turned. "By the way, did you notice the fellow in the
first compartment of this carriage?"

"The lanky fellow carrying the black bag?"

"That's the man."

"Yes. Interesting."

"Did you notice that his beard . . ."

"Is a fake?"

"And that he keeps touching his breast pocket . . ."

"As if he is terrified of losing something ex-
tremely valuable."

"The man is up to something, Morgan, and I believe he fears for his life. I should keep an eye on him
during your trans-Atlantic voyage were I you."

"I'd be happy to have your company. And your
help."

"No. I have other fish to fry. You don't need me.
You know my methods."

About the Author

H. PAUL JEFFERS is an executive with WCBS News-radio 88 in New York, an author, and a member of the Baker Street Irregulars. Among his books are *The Adventure of the Stalwart Companions,* a Sherlock Holmes story set in New York City in 1880, and *Rubout at the Onyx,* a hard-boiled detective story that unfolds on Fifty-second Street in New York in the mid-1930s when jazz is king.